UNCIVIL

DOMINIQUE ROBBINS

UNCIVIL

ISBN: 978-1-7353303-0-3

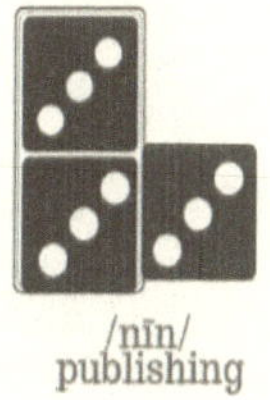

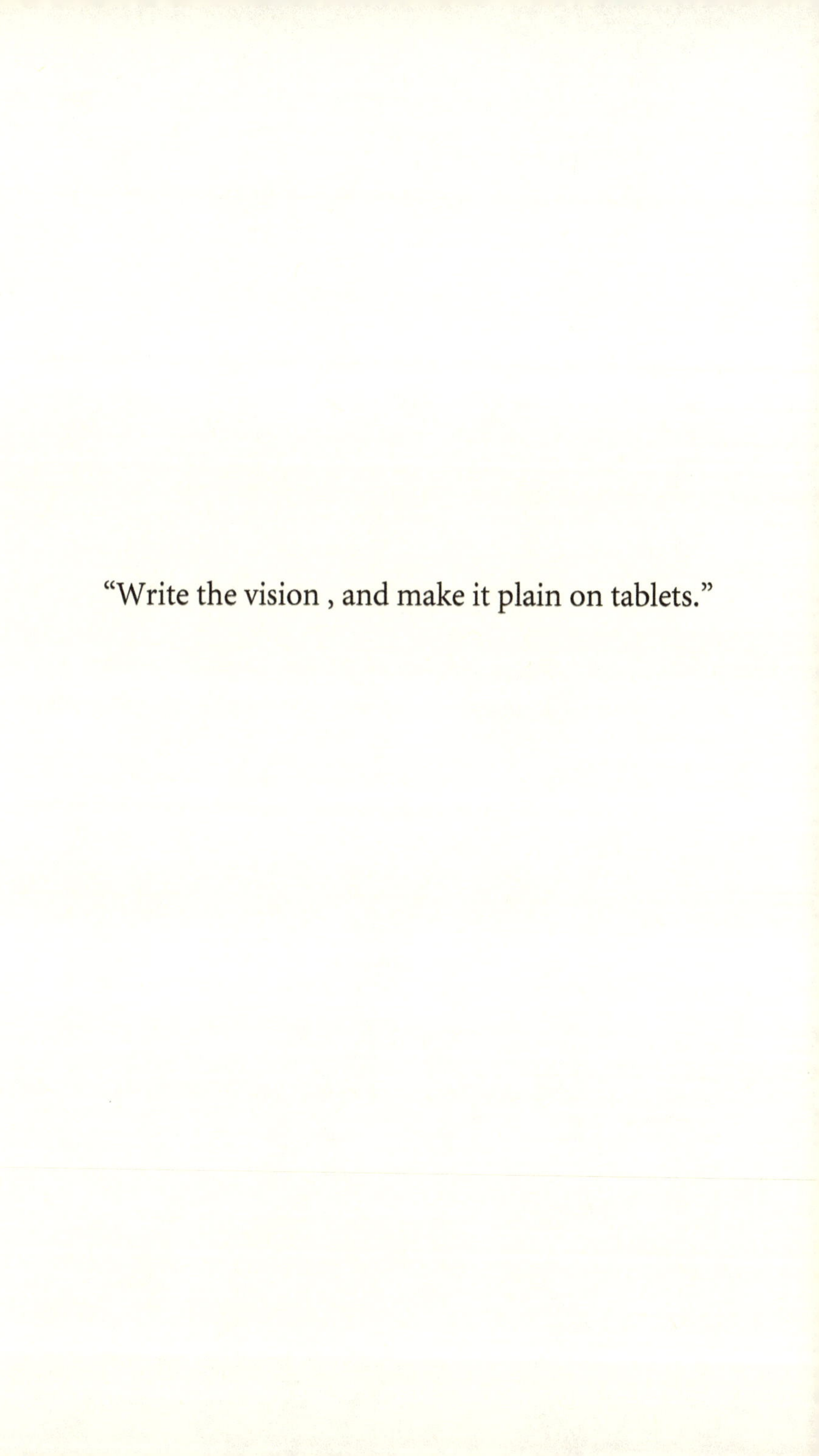

"Write the vision , and make it plain on tablets."

DEDICATION

This book was written for my daughter, Taylor. You are *good* in all the word's essence, and mightier than you know.

This milestone is dedicated to my soul sync Marquis. Thank you for your light and power and showing me the balance between strength and tenderness.

This narrative is dedicated to my mother, my family, and the ancestors whose shoulders I humbly stand on.

TABLE OF CONTENTS

PREFACE

WHILE THIS STORY AND ITS characters are disguised as fiction, its themes and subject matters are not. In choosing to read this narrative, you're choosing understanding and expansion. A willingness to see the slippery slope of rights infringement and how it impacts us all. While most stories depict societal collapse being the fault of plague, ominous nature, or zombies, I wanted to explore the human element. What happens when its society's fault and there is no longer exemption? Set in the aftermath of revolt, the characters, along with the old-era oppressors, are all made to struggle in survival; due to the lack of support given to marginalized people. This is a not-so-far-off future. Although dystopian in genre, I wrote this to urge those feeling despair that no matter how bad it gets we still have a future here, together. Our humanity and fierceness will be felt.

From July 2019 to March 2020, this novel has evolved and yet, it's still very relevant to the problems plaguing people of color dating back centuries and into the foreseeable future. The current crossroads we find ourselves in CAN be rerouted to a better destination. Don't allow our works and past advocacy to be in vain. Be encouraged. The future is ours.

This is for the fight.

–Dom

ONE

A FROZEN FRAME OF ACTION News' Jovita Morison stared into me, I stared back. I haven't seen a working digital screen in months. Her expression was soft, and my unconscious lulled me forward. Seeing someone without crisis in their eyes, soft.

"Keep looking!" The familiarity of Elise's voice brought me back to. I bagged the tablet, its charger, and all the electronics I could find. We weaved through each room with precision. Combing through every square foot of this suburban fortress for anything resembling aid to livelihood. My tinnitus began to rumble as the echoes of an M4 round entered my inner ear.

"We found one more!" Isaac asserted. I glanced down the stairwell and was met by a warm corpse with expensive taste, freshly dragged from the basement.

"Cool, burn her out back." I directed.

Would the smoke draw attention? Possibly, but did I care? Not in the least. We would be long gone by then. Burning the body was an act of good faith and respect to their soul, but more of a gesture of "fuck you" to The Scourge. I whistled to urge our impending departure. Packs thrown over backs, we loaded up. Two compact sedans and a SUV in tow, we moved cautiously through town en route to our wooded rally point. Everyone knows the drill. Obey all stop signs, windows up, drive slowly, bring no attention to yourself. These were protected zones. All of the public officials and Scourge affiliates lived here. Or scattered about in what was left of here. The Entry Controllers are so consumed in trafficking rogue citizens, they've left their territory vulnerable. Hmmph, great for us.

As we approached the highway on ramp, we took a sharp turn onto an access road. A quick scan, of the road behind and in front of us indicated no threat, as we advanced further. We drove in silence. Vigilance was key to survival. And how do you survive when everyone left is a top predator? Hide in plain sight and kill whatever isn't familiar.

Elise turned the wheel as we approached the peeling MATHEWS 721 addressed mailbox and drove down a winding driveway. Passing the towering pecan tree sparked the faintest memory of the first home we lived in, every time. We slowed past the stone-veneered cottage into its backyard brush. Well into the trees,

Elise navigated slowly along a barely visible trail. She knew the way, but that was no comfort. Every expedition caused more anxiety. Her eyes flickered to the corners, a side stare begging to be met. I placed my hand on the nape of her neck to give a stress-relieving squeeze. It wasn't enough. She exhaled hesitantly, letting me know she appreciated the effort. The car stopped short of a natural barricade. Snapped tree trunks and a shallow creek marked the second leg of our journey. We made it.

"Elise, start unloading, the others should be here soon," I said. As she went towards the trunk, I ejected the passenger chair to grab our haul of food and supplies out of the back seat. I approached the tailgate and we caught eyes again. "You okay?" I asked.

"Mostly," she reassured. Since we were kids, Elise has been a girl of few words. Our family always joked that if nothing else in life worked out, she could be a professional mime. Her smile would beam while she listened in on conversations, but words would rarely escape her lips. That was a lighter time, though. Elise was the baby of our siblings. She exhibited bits of us all but still reserved a regal mystery representative of her past self. Hardened by present times, I respected her ability to cope but resented her having to.

"Guess what I found?" I said, trying to lighten her mood. Her head raised curiously. I pulled a bag of opened sunflower seeds from my backpack. "I found it at the truck stop on the way in. Figured it would be a good celebration gift once we made it out." The corner of her mouth creased as I handed it to her. Just as I unclipped my gun harness, Dani, Lamor, and Kayson pulled in.

"Isaac and Freya aren't too far behind," Kayson said, exiting their vehicle.

"What do you think?" Dani gloated, showcasing a diamond bracelet.

"Glad to see you're focused," I said. "How does that help the reserve?"

She dismissed me with a look and threw a bag at my feet. I shifted it with my foot enough to hear the clinks of pots and utensils. Lamor did what he always did, ignored her. One by one Kayson checked each vehicle's tread, mirrors, backup arsenal in the floors, and fuel levels. He did this every time we went out of the reserve. His eyes were usually the first and last set to examine our transportation. And I wouldn't have it any other way.

Without words, it was muscle memory as he gassed up the vehicles with our fuel cans. Elise was outfitting each car with loose brush. Lamor went on towards the driveway to close the tree gap as Freya and Isaac rolled in. Isaac hopped out prematurely and he and Lamor dusted up our tracks.

We did our best to remain invisible. That's how we survived. We traveled back to the reserve in silence, on foot, per usual. Vigilance couldn't be accomplished otherwise. The downside of that silence was being trapped in our minds where sorrow and fear hid. Traveling beyond our camp was only done in non-routine cycles. Either entirely on foot or by vehicle, groups took one of two paths on or off the reserve, then branched off from there. Varying the routes and method of travel kept us from creating noticeable trails. Everyone knew, you only leave in groups to gather medicine or objects for community advancement, nothing more, nothing else. We voted to decide what was worth risking exposure and our lives. If we get lucky, food, books, or other luxuries were found along the way.

The Scourge was snatching up more people, last we'd heard. I figure it's a half-ass attempt at saving this poor world that we created. Nonetheless, it made every mission and every journey more dangerous. The problem is you never know who is for you or against you. Opposition to the cause itself or interpersonal, your enemy remains unknown.

Over a year ago, our civil liberties began to disappear and have more qualifiers. It began with the doubling down of the Thirteenth Amendment, arresting people for anything and everything to get more free labor. This disproportionately affected blacks, browns and, hell, the dark adjacent. You could never be seen as unarmed if you were born black. That blackness was a weapon and gave society, especially cops a license to kill. News networks would race bait with splashy headlines, when the truth wasn't as trendy or provocative. Deaths were seen as deserved whether playing while black as a child, driving while black as a women, or jogging while black as a man. In every form, in any scenario, persons of interest weren't held accountable. The digital age gave the world access to visuals of already existing facts. Yet somehow accountability became a luxury. Trained professionals were allowed to fear for their lives but those with barrels aimed in their direction or with obstructed airways needed to remain calm.

We were treated as less than for centuries, having secured basic American rights only 60 years ago. Yet when we are upset by the egregious acts, we're stereotyped as angry or the aggressor.

When digital boycott and awareness wasn't enough, we protested. A few laws changed here and there with blanket pacification: condemning voter suppression, labeling lynching a hate crime, enforcing body cameras that were controlled by the wearing officer.

None of which was enough to stop the murders and mass incarceration of black people that lingered without consequence. When protesting grew tiresome the people grew fierce. Neighborhoods deployed armed watch groups to protect themselves against over-policing. Community programs rooted in law, finances, and history launched to begin economic empowerment. It was like another Harlem Renaissance. Soon government groups labeled the movement as a cult and radical. Using singular acts of violence to add substance to their claims. When some southern states decided to deploy the national guard, the people struck back. Throwing rocks as warnings and bricks as weapons, it only took two standoffs and infinite lines of armed men and women for them to see we wouldn't back down. The Council of Presidents decided to supersede political balances with an executive order: banning all firearms.

The revocation of the Second Amendment under the guise of national protection; yeah, that upset the whites.

This had an unintended ripple effect into the same white groups that once condemned our rebellion. When gun surrender points started appearing in every county countrywide, the protest and panic got worse.

Back then a law could only be an executive order for a month before being voted on to be kept. However that was still too long. Before the vote could be brought to ballot, a bill was passed through legislation, revoking voter eligibility.

When proof of lineage became a qualifier of voting and natural residency. Everyone on the rainbow spectrum between black and tanned white were deemed ineligible, some even investigated for deportation.

This overturning of the Fourteenth Amendment upset everyone in between.

America, like an ugly fungus, still somehow maintained a mycelia network of racist redlining and a heritage of oppression. Only the lines were blurred against more than just us.

Some who had the luxury of political associations and power, or pure ignorance, didn't see a problem with the executive order. It went from solely a race issue to a class issue. If you were of color OR middle class, you were a legislative target. They tried to tell us how to respond to our oppression. Protest, but peacefully. Demand justice, but ask civilly. It's not up to anyone to tell a group how they should rebel against their own genocide. Anything other than ally-ism was taking up space.

Although, with the numbers of our allies swelling, tensions grew in daily life. Simple acts like going to work and grocery shopping couldn't be done without observing the people around you. Unfortunately, being confronted by political enemies with unwavering indifference towards your struggle, stirred instant conflict. Everyone lived on edge with constant policing and cyber-monitoring. When talks of revolt became magnified on social platforms, everything seethed over.

Noticeably, more people were hashtagging #PrayforUS. Across socials, profile pictures and avis swapped for green tiles to represent the renewal we all desperately needed and the political balance the oppressed sought. Spouts of violence within communities took over headlines, and the protests that followed were all but peaceful. More prominent people began speaking out, other countries gave their input, and the nation picked sides. Rich, poor, Democrat, or Republican, everyone tiptoed to their side of the divide and remained steadfast in their position.

Middle class neighborhoods were torched as an intimidation tactic. Community members began hiding away in safe houses, to remain unseen from retaliation. We all were angry but not everyone wanted to fight. A second attempt to deploy troops to domestic locations quickly failed. Somehow the government forgot those troops were people, before they were soldiers. And half of their men and women were directly affected by the new era and couldn't support the crumbling government's "new mission."

Without regard for tyrant authority or those who kept the order, society ran unsanctioned.

Canada foresaw what was to come and erected a border wall. Mexico then reinforced theirs. California even appealed to the United Nations to be an independent territory from the United States and be recognized as a bordering country. The ruling of the U.N.'s vote and the U.S.A. resignation of territory remains unknown. However, the rumored army that California created indicates their own "ruling." By the time the rebellion broke out, all cyber and cellular communication had been cut. Not a post to be shared to tell the story of misfortune and violence Americans suffered through. Social standing bled over into real life, with a green X painted on homes, being the lasting indicator of your alignment with human rights. This was both good and bad depending on those who saw it. You were either an ally or a target. No help was coming. Society grasped at what they could for salvation: each other, religion, and the misdirected policies of the former government. What's more troubling is whether Scourge sympathizers really believed in the tyrant-driven agenda or did they align themselves to avoid being collateral damage?

Church took over state in the new era. People were performing rituals in Scourge communities for forgiveness. As if God was still betting on us.

Perception was reality these days. And to those we called the Scourge, we were uncivil.

TWO

THE REFUGE WAS AN OLD youth summer camp, one in the mountains of Georgia. Across fourteen cabins and two rec facilities converted to community common space, we thrived the best we could in this day. Further down the interstate we had an outpost within an under-developed subdivision. And by subdivision, I mean two cul-de-sacs. A few of us thought it'd be smart to have a secondary safe haven. We stored some canned goods there, amongst other necessities.

Their eyes were everywhere but so were ours. We had allies near and far, each with a different cause to stand on. The common denominator was that none of us would accept divisiveness or control. Although we risked exposure if we lived collectively, we looked out for each other from afar and provided shelter in long travels.

"Ayeee" echoes as a resounding hello. Finally, I exhaled. We resurfaced to a clearing beyond the brush of our reserve. To most, these woods looked like a dense web of branches. But to the skilled survivalists, its shady borough was perfect to escape the grasp of elitist Scourgers. Lucky for us, even the hardiest of conservative outdoorsmen didn't appreciate their guns being taken away. They are with us, and are the few bold enough to navigate this side of nature.

"What did you bring us?" some of the children failed to whisper.

Dani kneeled to Lynn, "We didn't have time to scavenge, babe." Before Lynn could finish her frown, Dani pulled out a frisbee and a lavender headband she adjusted slyly on Lynn's head. A rolling giggle erupted from the tiny humans and they scattered towards the lake.

"I'm going to go get started on supper," Kayson said. Elise headed straight for our cabin.

I hesitantly followed. "Are you sure you're o—"

"I'm fine," she retorted.

I let it stand. "I'm going to head over to the galley to give everyone a hot wash of today," I said. She nodded.

Dani was in the galley before me. She organized some of our findings into piles with similarities.

Handsets and receivers from old landlines and radios. Another table labeled consignment for community members to bring clothes they've outgrown, to pass down. Utensils for food or to aid during crop season. And items for security. Makeshift traps and alarms for our reserve perimeter; ammunition and firearms for the people.

We were positioned on a lake with just enough runoff from the Etowah River to keep from having dormant waters. The lake made bathing and cooking easier, as well as tactical positioning as opposed to the alternative. Redeye bass populated our waterway. Thankfully so, considering that game was hard to come by. The days have become hotter and the ecosystem has adjusted accordingly.

Sitting outside the galley on a stump, I inhaled sharply. Looking out at everything our community has built and their daily commitment to survival gave me grief. I'm sure we all grieved our old lives at one time or another. It was a rarity for me, though. Compliments of my PTSD, I stored away any harmful memories far in the corner closet of my mind. Dr. Van says it's a form of coping. An emotional cocktail of indifference and numbness kept me from our sobering reality of societal crumble. In previous years, the combination of water and towering trees would be a serene escape. I tried to piece together that feeling through moments like this; observing from my stump and smelling earth's essence.

The cracking of pine needles under footsteps neared, making me more aware of the present. The galley was filling. Lamor was in the front situating the elders. Freya hovered nearby as Isaac was scribbling notes, glancing up to scan the room every so often. Dani was collecting shirts. Elise postured in the second row, elbows on knees, leaning into her thoughts. I walked up the aisle giving reassuring nods and smiles along the way. I gave Lamor a loose knuckle pound and the town hall meeting began.

"All right, how's everyone doing today?" I pried rhetorically. "As you know, before dawn a few of us set out to retrieve what we could for the med group," I continued. "We hit an old dialysis clinic and gathered enough minor injury supplies to last the year."

Isaac then inserted, "Mrs. Geter, raise your hand please. Mrs. Geter will need three volunteers to assist in counting inventory and putting it away. Please, those of you who have been apprenticing with medical, get with her and Lamor after this."

Elise and my eyes met. I urged her, in stare, to join us in the front. She refused with a blink.

Dani added, "Moving on, we also went a little southeast to old 7b." One community member met her announcement with a humph, while others released a sigh of concern.

Zone 7b was what used to be Alpharetta. When the divide first took place, they tried to kick out anyone deemed uncivil. A lot of people there were too rich to care about "our issues," until the "our" also became "them." By the time they tried to rectify wrongs, it was too late, word spread. They were labeled sympathetic to the Scourge and eventually armored themselves in the reputation.

"Listen," I began. "We got a tip from 11D that someone on the outskirts of Scourge limits had communications equipment. While the initial vote to leave the reserve wasn't based on this discovery, we took a field measure and embraced the risk."

Lamor echoed, "Per usual, our boys downtown had good info. We found some old satellite phones. A couple UHF radios and antenna parts."

"The radios may need some work, but nothing we can't figure out to get them up and running," Freya added.

Dani smirked, "Even found solar chargers and a tablet with some educational videos saved. The kids can check it out of the study."

The room's grumbling died down. "We now have better ability to communicate with each other and our network. To us, the mission warranted some improvising," I concluded.

The twisted expression of Spittle caught my attention, Freya's too. "What's up, Spit?" she directed into the audience.

"Nothin'," he teased. "Just doing the math on how long the tech team will be up tonight shooting blanks at these radios." A laughing roar erupted.

Freya humored him, "Long enough for me to carry your ass through the troubleshooting phase." She threw a pencil, which he caught and placed behind his ear.

Elise smirked. "We can get started as early as tomorrow on installing some of the solar panels," she said. "With some of the power supplies we rigged up, we can have a head start on winter with stored reserve power for heaters."

Elder Glen turned in her chair to face her, "We are very grateful for you Elise." They shared a smile. She placed her fragile hand out and Elise enclosed it within hers. With a gentle kiss, she released her hand and sat back in her chair.

Caught in the moment, I almost forgot to ask, "How many people will you need initially?"

Elise stood. "I'll need five able-bodied people to begin roof renovation and running cable. Any youth who can wield a shovel to dig cable trenches, bring them as well. I expect it to take ten days, give or take." Elise sat back down.

"Before we close the hot wash does anyone have anything to add?" Isaac fished.

Dani raised a hand. "If anyone has clothes they've grown out of, or needs items for winter, please see me after. Also, tonight is red beans and rice so get it while there's gravy."

"And be sure to thank Kayson for his culinary resourcefulness, guys," Isaac said, sternly.

"I got something. Did anyone find any Oreo cookies or Fluff while y'all were out?" Spittle joked. "I'm not sure how long morale can stay up without it."

"All right, goodnight everybody," I hollered over laughs and chair leg scrapes.

The crowd thinned, leaving Isaac, Freya, and I lingering behind. "So, Nixon, what's the plan for tomorrow?" I looked up to see Isaac and Freya staring back.

"We gotta look into that other thing 11D told us about," I said.

"And if it's true?" questioned Isaac.

"Then we burn this place down and be done with it," I said sharply.

THREE

M Y FLAT WAS CLOSEST TO the perimeter. I figured if we ever had an intrusion I'd be the first to encounter our enemies. It was less of a protective measure for the group and more of a selfish countermeasure. Nobody, including Elise, could have my back like I had my back. Being on the offensive kept me prepared. It kept me hyper-alert; accepting whatever came with it. Mostly though, I enjoyed the detachment. Especially, at night where the world dimmed and a calming aura came with it.

Psithurism, a noun. Meaning the sound of tree leaves rustling.

I enjoyed psithurism, accompanied by whistles of wind that slid between mountains. It was nature not competing with mankind and our noise, both literally and figuratively.

The next morning, I woke up with the sun. Mind more awake than my body, my eyes blurred to focus on the screen door separating me from the environment.

With a balled fist, I tried to knead away the tightness in my chest, as I got up. Anxiety washed over me. Every morning, my heart pounded in my ribcage. I became overwhelmingly anxious. I walked over to the bowl on my dresser and splashed water in my face. Routines and certainty were the only things proven to disarm an anxiety attack. However, in this current state I could only have one. I recited my routine in my head as I went on to the next steps. Canteen on sling, I grabbed my toothbrush and stepped outside, careful not to wake Elise. I brushed grit from my teeth and tongue, swigged a gulp of water and spit. Events of the day prior replayed in my mind as I rearranged them like puzzle pieces.

11D was eleven degrees south of us. Between Freya, Isaac, and I, we were familiar with a good number of people through our bulletins and trusted them, too. We shared a common outpost community with their group and a pit stop we used to replenish ourselves on missions. It also made a good bulletin board for us to communicate messages without being face to face. I read and reread this crinkled page ripped from a magazine. The page number was underlined, with the number one scribbled next to it meaning: This is our first correspondence on the topic. We rarely wrote past three threads of communication. On the backside in between paragraph lines read.

7b has comm. gear. Find greenhouse 174 Culver. Relocate your group. Leave nothing behind.

"Relocate group… leave nothing behind," I read out loud. I grabbed a page of tarnished newspaper and underlined the page number writing 2 next to it meaning: response to your topic. Thread 2: "Relocate why? What do you know" I started to write. Though, before I did, I paused. *How urgent was this message?* I thought. Nothing I could write covered all the questions I was left with. I put on a shirt to go outside and walked towards the lake, hoping to find Isaac. Very few were awake let alone wandering at this hour but I knew Isaac would be. In his words "There's always something to be done." In both daily life and seemingly impossible situations, it rang true. That mentality ensured his early rising to make his day as productive as possible.

Barely off the shore, I faced our camp and scanned the tree line. After a few seconds, I gave up until catching him in my peripheral at the far end of the shore. I guess I looked as disheveled as my thoughts when I approached; Isaac asked, "You good?"

"Yeah, yeah I'm fine man. Just can't understand 11D's message," I said.

Isaac looked down and shook his head. "Yeah Nixon, it's uh. It's a tough one. We have a good thing going here. For once in a very long time people are feeling secure. We're just supposed to uproot that? Over some vague intel?"

I could hear the contempt in his voice. He was right. I hated to admit it. Normally veering on the side of caution, I would suggest immediate movement. Yet, I didn't want to put everyone back into crisis mode. However, we couldn't bring this thread to them without certainty. It would only cause worry. If nothing else, one thing we seemed to get right was communication. We've created a culture on our reserve of transparency and community. We couldn't make a decision for everyone. Moreover, we couldn't bring them unverified gossip either.

"When the others wake up, let's tell them about the second part of the message," I began. "Then we can try to make sense of this whole thing." Isaac nodded.

I helped Isaac secure the rest of his lines to tree branches to get a jumpstart on the afternoon catch. Hooked with earthworms and other insects, we walked away confident. "How's Angelique?" I firmly tapped his arm.

"She's doing pretty good, considering," he said.

Isaac was married to the love of his life. It was a beautiful reminder of humanity. She, dynamic and kind, was just as ambitious as he was. She had a strong hold on camp structure and gave incredible effort, keeping everyone productive and cared for.

We approached Isaac's cabin where Angelique sat on the steps. She looked up from cleaning the bolt chamber of her gun to meet us with a warm smile. "Hey, Nix. How're you feeling?" she said, before embracing me. I reciprocated lightly to avoid her protruding baby bump.

"I'm good, Angie. How's the little one?" She kissed both of my cheeks.

"You know, giving her mama a little attitude already. Her kicks kept me up half the night."

Isaac rubbed her stomach lovingly. "Wonder where she gets that from?" He said, smiling at me, looking for a co-sign. I looked at Angelique and quickly reconsidered. We all laughed.

"So Nixon, am I going to see you in group after breakfast?" asked Angelique.

"Not today, but save me a seat next time." In an attempt to sound as reassuring as possible, I added, "We're pretty busy this week, but I'll be sure to sit with Dr. Van one-on-one at some point. Promise." Isaac looked away. Angelique looked like her bullshit meter was surging.

"We're going to head over to see Elise, do you need anything before I go?" He said. Angelique scowled, Isaac kissed her on the cheek and began walking away cueing me to do the same.

"Man, could you do me a favor and not annoy my wife!?" Isaac was serious yet humored. "Now, I'm going to hear about why I'm not being a better friend and making sure you're taking care of yourself. We've all got shit, Nix, the difference is you're not dealing with yours."

All I could do was nod. Dr. Van made it a point to hold group counseling once a week for each age group. The kids drew and played games to learn healthy communication. Teens and young adults worked through their angst and resentment of the world we left them. The middle-aged and parents discussed our daily pressures of keeping everyone safe and balancing our own mental health. Then the elders prayed and convened on when and what wisdom to impart on us all. Being that they have lived through tumultuous times in this country before, they were most optimistic of the resulting outcome. We leaned on them to keep us focused and informed. A priceless commodity in recent days.

Walking towards a former RV campground we found Elise prepping for the day's work. "Morning," Isaac sung out.

"Morning guys," she said.

"Whatcha got in the works?" I asked looking over her shoulder. Elise was working steadily on a draft that looked like a platform. She was studying to become and architect and was damn good in carpentry thanks to our grandad. She moved here to go to school and be closer to me, leaving our family and grandpa back in

Florida. He shown through her anytime she began a new construction project.

"I was thinking of putting the panels higher up in the canopy to absorb as much sunlight as possible. If we leave them on the ground, we'll only get four hours of prime sunlight before the tree lines block it during rise and set." Her tone was informative and sure. Knowing her, Isaac and I knew the subject was hers to govern. She spoke with intent and very rarely required further deliberation. "Once the platform is constructed, the main concern is running lines that can't be damaged by the elements or people. If we run them underground and use extension cords from power source to panel we will be good to go. I'm going to get with Spittle later to figure out the best way to connect each housing unit, via the roofs, to the power panel."

I smiled. "Awesome, so if we only connect at night we can power the heaters, stay warm, but still preserve enough power for everyone to use for emergency cold weather conditions in peak season."

"Exactly," Elise summarized.

"So what can we do Eli?" Isaac asked.

"Chop wood, we're going to need a lot of it," she pointed to an axe on the ground.

Isaac and I took turns chopping pieces of wood. We assembled bushels of tree branches to act as foundation shoring. Elise started collecting pieces of the wood we chopped and hammered them into the tree trunk upward to the branch collar. The beginnings of a ladder was completed.

By the time we reached a good stopping point we noticed more bodies moving about the reserve and it was time for breakfast. As we walked towards the galley I started to tell Elise about the second half of the note. She looked at the ground as we walked and simply replied, "I know." Before I could ask how, she finished. "When could you ever hide something from me? I knew something was up when Isaac and Freya started whispering at the truck stop." She got me.

"Alright, well what do you say? What should we do about it?"

"It's really not up to me now is it?" her pace quickened, leaving me a few steps behind as we entered the galley. Immediately, I spotted Kayson handing out peaches and scoops of oatmeal. I grabbed one of the many mismatched bowls and joined the receiving line.

"Good morning, Elise, Isaac, Nixon." Kayson greeted us independently. His deep voice faded into a closed mouth grin. "Good morning, Sonny. How are you doing brother?" Isaac responded genuinely.

"I woke up, today's already great." Kayson said. It was the same thing he said every day. Kayson was an older middle-aged guy and a man of habit.

Up until the revolt, Kayson was a drunk. A man who had given up on the world and himself. He had a daughter young and had no contact with her other than a single direct message updating him on her life, her child, and confirming her disdain for him. He hit rock bottom more than once but the last straw was not knowing whether his kid was alive after the dust settled. The guilt evolved into depression and grief. Lucky for him, he and Dr. Van crossed paths early on. Isaac and I spotted them and a few others in Dr. Van's condo downtown. From the street it was an eye soar, curtains drawn and a dim light hidden behind. Back then there was safety in numbers, but left untrained, those numbers could get you killed.

We headed up with caution and found eight people disheveled, hidden in a bedroom where it appeared they all slept. Uncertain of our intentions, they had tear-filled eyes awaiting what was next. We put our weapons away and introduced ourselves. We explained how we found them and the error in being so visible. Dr. Van stood and inquired why we bothered coming up. To which Isaac replied, "Because we thought you may be one of us. But, if y'all were those scourging bastards, we wasn't gonna let you expand your lungs another second." Dr. Van just nodded and offered us a drink.

Kayson stood, looked me dead in the eyes and said, "So show us. Show us how to survive this." They each spoke with such conviction but Kayson, he spoke as though losing another battle wasn't an option.

I trusted them both, and my instincts were rarely wrong. We offered for them to come with us to our camp, and urged them to only take what they could carry. For some, that was their small child. During the journey, I even saw Sonny carrying a little one from time to time. The trip was a little over an hour drive but took all day having walked a good portion. Despite the increase in numbers, we still couldn't risk being followed in a vehicle or ambushed while taking main highways. We bobbed and weaved through neighborhoods, woods, and industrial districts. Dr. Van and Kayson took the lead of their people and kept their spirits as high as they could. Ever sense, I've leaned on the both of them and have been grateful for their presence on the reserve. Having a second chance at life, Kayson has made it a point to care for the people around him. He cooks most meals, helps keep camp organized, and oversees most camp safety measures without a complaint. And every day for the last few months, waking up has been the only prerequisite for having a good day.

In Kayson's presence, I couldn't help but smile. Elise initiated the show of gratitude, "Thank you for breakfast, Sonny." We each echoed the sentiment. He graciously obliged as we walked towards a table. Once seated, I searched Elise's face waiting for acknowledgment to pick up our conversation.

"El." Her eyebrow raised. "Elise, I know, I'm not saying we should decide. I'm only asking what do you think of the message. I fully intend on bringing it to the group for a vote."

"Well, I have no opinion then," Elise dismissed. "Nothing is permanent. I mean, this was never a long-term solution realistically. If we gotta go, we gotta go."

I hated hearing how coarse she sounded. I wish she felt more optimistic about the future. Although, I quickly realized how hard an ask that was.

"Okay, well," I lowered my voice. "If it is good intel. That means the scourge is targeting us."

Isaac chimed in, "Then, the other option is to stay. And fight." He looked at me, then back at Elise. She tried to control her expression but her eyes had already widened. "It's not the best option, but it is an option. I personally think our best bet is to uproot."

I lowered my voice another octave. "Yes we have the arms and we have been training a few of our people on how to protect themselves. But that was for defense not offense." My attention shifted to Isaac as he spoke.

"In order to win a potential battle, all we need is the element of surprise. It would be easy to switch gears if we know they're coming," he said. I felt guilty agreeing to such a thing. I knew Angelique was pregnant and was his world. Of course I didn't want harm to come to her, she was my friend too. But I knew a life on the run wasn't what Isaac wanted for himself or his family, even if it was too risky to say out loud.

Elise took two more bites of oatmeal. She wiped her mouth with her sleeve and stated, "Gwen." Isaac and I both shared expressions of inquiry. Elise finished, "Talk to Elder Gwen, she could be the beacon of insight you have yet to consider." She got up from her seat, ending the conversation. She was right. Although I'm not certain that this exact piece of history is repeating itself, I think Elder Gwen has some historic references on how to move forward. Isaac snapped me out of my thought haze,

"That sister of yours." Isaac laughed.

"Yeah man, been calling me on my shit since 2004, baby babble and all." We hurdled over the bench towards the kitchen to wash our bowls and head over to Elder Gwen's cabin.

Isaac tread lightly on the front steps of Elder Gwen's place and gently knocked on the screen door; although, she could see us and we her through the mesh barrier, we indulged in respectful niceties.

"Come on in boys," Gwen said joyfully. "To what do I owe the occasion?" Lamor was there taking her vitals. Her demeanor was of no indication, but her health wasn't the best.

"What's going on fellas?" Lamor acknowledged us warmly.

"Hey man, I'm glad you're here, but we came to ask for some advice, from Mrs. Gwen." I gestured to her.

"Well?" she said impatiently.

I divulged, "Well on the mission yesterday, we stopped at one of our pitstops. 11D had initiated a new thread about the reserve and us staying here. We can't make sense of the message or figure out what to do about it."

She remained seated, quiet in thought before she replied, "Let me see it." Intuitively she knew I wouldn't show up without it. I pulled the folded paper out of my pocket and handed it to Elder Gwen. Lamor positioned himself alongside her to have a better reading view. Her hand raised to cover her mouth, as if holding in a silent gasp. Lamor looked at me, both of us waiting for the silence to be broken. "What can you control Nixon?" she asked. I stared, confused. She folded the old newspaper into quarters before repeating herself. "What can you control?"

At this point I heard the rhetorical nature of the question.

Her monologue soon flowed. "Emotion is a fickle thing. It is never consistent or trustworthy." Her hand reached out to Lamor to help her up. "Emotions are reactions to people or situations based on the correlation you have with it. The thing that makes you laugh may make someone else cry. Emotions aren't consistent, and while they are valid for every individual person, they are not rooted in fact. Moreover, they are not rooted in truth." She exited her cabin with us all in tow. "Nixon, do you know why you don't know how to approach this situation?"

My sarcasm thought, *If I knew WHY I didn't know, I wouldn't be here,* but respect couldn't allow that to leave me lips. I simply listened more intently. Elder Gwen faced me, halting us all in our tracks.

"You have no approach because you have no truth. This message struck fear in you," pointing at Isaac and I. "Fear of possible danger, fear of losing everything you built, fear of death. So many emotions. I'm guessing you two want to pick up and leave?" She corrected herself. "No, this one, you want to fight." She pointed to Isaac. I suddenly felt slight shame. "Both of you are valid in your feelings, but where's the truth? Why did they send this message and what do they know that you don't? These are questions you need to ask. But you need to ask them. That's where the truth lies: between perspective and information." We all sunk into ourselves for not prioritizing it sooner.

All I could mutter was, "Yes ma'am."

"We'll let everyone know we have an emergency town hall tonight. If the votes incline, we'll plan for a mission to 11D two days from now," said Isaac.

There goes that tightness in my chest. Unescapable pressure acted as a door that my fears pounded on the other side of. Lamor and Isaac carried on a conversation a few steps ahead of me as we walked away from Elder Gwen's. My mind raced with every possible scenario ranging from rational to utter terror. How risky is it to go back out so soon? Did we have enough time to send a new thread and receive a reply without being ambushed? Probably not.

Dragging towards my cabin, I steadied myself. I was nervous Elise would be there, able to read my mood on arrival. To my relief, as I approached the screen door I saw she wasn't back yet. My old mattress creaked as I sat down. As well-acquainted as I was with war, why should we willingly fight? I didn't understand how such circumstances could follow me back here, to the states. Going to 11D was, at minimum, risky. We could be followed, or worse, hunted? My imagination took me into golden hour as the sun began to set. Somehow my body relaxed enough to lay horizontally but stayed stressed enough to keep me awake.

"Are YOU alright?" Elise asked as she entered the cabin. She knew.

"You knew what Gwen would say, didn't you?"

"How could I, Nix? I just thought she had insight to offer. And I was right. Even if it wasn't what you wanted to hear." Her tone faded off.

"You're okay with this? Going so far off the reserve, putting ourselves in jeopardy again? We decided against things like this in the beginning El, we have rule—"

"Rules!" she shrieked. "Is that what you were going to say? Rules? We live in a lawless world now brother, wake up! So rules for what exactly, to keep us safe, to keep our people safe? You wanting to do the right thing is what brought most of these people here. It's not your responsibility to save everyone, you just made it that way. Is going to 11D ideal, no. But what's the alternative. Getting worked up over something that may or may not be a threat?" With every question she posed, I grew more ambivalent. There was no way around the risk in front of us.

Just then Freya knocked. "Hey guys, I hope I'm not interrupting," knowing that she was. "Some of us wanted to get together before the big meeting. We're all over in my cabin"

Elise turned around and riffled through her near empty drawer. "We'll be down," she muttered.

Freya left without another word. As much as Elise had yelled at me, I knew her too well to take offense. I aligned myself next to her, both of us facing the wall. I took advantage of the small space between us and rocked enough to give her a nudge. She smirked. I cradled two fingers under her chin and lifted her head up; a silent affirmation between us. Her head rose and she shifted her thick loose hair, barely tucking it behind her ears. Each time she did this, it was as if she put on an invisible cape. Immediately, she turned around to make her exit. I instinctively followed.

Kayson was on the steps when we arrived at Freya's, he patted my back as I passed him on our way to join the others inside. On one side a workbench, on the other, a bed. Isaac, Lamor, Dani, and Freya were all huddled together.

As Elise, Kayson and I found space to settle, Isaac began. "As most of you know by now, we got a thread from 11D urging us to leave camp, but we don't know why." Few faces looked surprised. "I know we all talk. We weren't keeping this a secret but trying to manage its spread before we had solutions of what to do next." Lamor nodded to Isaac in consent. He continued, "Nixon and I spoke to Elder Gwen earlier today. We thought she may be able to give us some clarity; as usual, she delivered. She suggested that we travel to 11D and get to the root of the message and find out what exactly they know that we don't."

Coughing, I cleared my throat. "Isaac and I shared some ideas. Elder Gwen shared hers, but what we want to know is, what do you all think?" The room remained silent, other than the gears turning in all of our minds. I decided to fill the space. "I struggled with this today, the same way I'm sure you all are now. But I may have a solution that settles some of our concerns. What if a few of us did go to the rail yard, but some of us stayed?"

Dani piped in, "To be sittin' ducks? Why would we leave camp halfcocked with only a few defenses AND leave some of us vulnerable en route to 11D?" I could hear her concern.

"No Dani, what I am saying is, if some go we are risking less lives. Then those who stay, can prepare the rest." I paused briefly. "Think about it, we've got a better chance if we have all hands capable of defending themselves. Those who stay can help by doing labs on how to use a gun or track or set traps. Everyone here contributes and that's great, but we need all our people self-reliant. We've been living as if our world is going to be kind again. As if humanity is still in play, but off of this reserve, they won't have time to discern who's against them." I hated hearing myself, although I knew it had to be said. "Elders and children included, each able person should be prepared to defend themselves and this camp. At first I wanted to flee, it seemed to be our best option. However, this intel being valid or not, we won't continue to be terrorized. We stay, we prepare. That's what I think."

Freya tilted her head, "That's not a terrible idea, but who stays and who goes?"

Kayson said firmly, "I'll go."

To which Dani chimed, "I'm in."

I instantly felt gratitude for how selfless they were. Humanity still lived here if nowhere else.

"I'm going to go, I can do more good there than here," I said. "Since this isn't a usual mission, we only need two or three people. Dani, the kids love you and you're great at hunting. You may be our best bet for teaching them tracking and trap setting." She agreed.

Freya said, "Normally, I'd be in, but I'm so close with these radios." Everyone understood.

Isaac asked, "Do you think you'll have one functioning by Sunday?"

Freya looked confused. "Yes, but even so you couldn't use it. You'd still need—" she paused, biting her lip. We all stared on. "I'll be back," she said and quickly ran off.

"Kayson man, what's everybody going to eat without you?" Lamor joked, "They'd have to rely on Mrs. Welsh." We shared a laugh. Kayson knew he was right.

"Well, you got me brother—" Isaac assured.

I cut him off, "Ahh no, Angelique isn't going to blame me for you leaving camp twice in one week."

"Have you seen her with a rifle. She doesn't need protecting, never has." He smiled to himself.

Lamor then concluded, "Either way, if you go or not, ask her if she'd be willing to show some folks their way around a weapon. If everyone was as confident with handling one, maybe this wouldn't be such a tough conversation."

Isaac responded, "You're right, I'll ask her when we're done here." I looked at Elise who was pinned against the door frame silent. Focusing over her shoulder, I could see Freya and Spittle in the distance. Her back faced me, but I could see Spittle in front of her, arms folded, hand over mouth.

Elise's eyes caught mine when she announced, "I'm going." I couldn't begin my objection by the time she finished saying, "We have how many months until winter? Those solar panels don't require my immediate attention and this is more important. I'm going."

Isaac side-barred with Lamor, when Freya reemerged. "I'm sending Spittle," she said proudly. "He can handle himself and he knows electronics."

"Why is that relevant?" Dani asked.

"Because," Freya said. "I'm sending whoever goes, with a uhf transceiver." She read some confusion in the room. "A radio, a walkie talkie, sort of. It can call out or receive a call transmission. I can have one ready to go by morning. If I send Spit, he can maintain it to ensure no issues, while they're out and hand deliver it to 11D instead of dropping it off at the pitstop. AND he can show them how to use it so we can stay in contact."

"That's great but what about the other radios?" Kayson asked.

"I'm still going to get them up and running." Freya said. "In the interim you guys should also take this." She handed me a portable boombox. I knew she had more to explain, so I waited. "Most of the airways are free so if you manually set it to 175.00 MHz you'll be able to hear whoever keys it with little static. It's not ideal, but after you drop the transceiver off, you'll at least be able to receive a message from 11D in case anything comes up. You just won't be able to talk back." I caught on to her train of thought.

"And if we leave Sunday and take another two days to make it to the rail yard, that'll give you enough time to get the other transceiver going." I added.

"Exactly." Freya beamed at the thought. "On your way back, once I get the other radio working, we'll be able to key in the same frequency and talk to you guys on mission and 11D directly."

Spittle walked in, "Hey sweet thang, what I miss? I hear you want my, services." He swayed towards Isaac with his lips puckered. He and Isaac threw playful punches and suddenly the mood in the room felt lighter. We stayed a few minutes longer to coordinate before the town hall meeting. I felt better about our best option. Moreover, I felt confident in it.

Hopefully, the camp will too.

FOUR

AFTER THE MEETING, I FELT… okay. Not happy, not angry or afraid, just okay. Over the next few days I knew we had to prepare for what felt like our most dangerous departure yet. Everyone was so well-spoken during the town hall about the issues we faced. In doing so, they instilled confidence in the rest of the reserve and successfully masked their own doubts. After a nearly-unanimous vote, I had to own that, I underestimated everyone's willingness to arm up and protect what we've built. However, I expected nothing short of what occurred, when the votes supported *us* going back out. Eventually, I resigned to the idea that Elise would be coming along and it slowly became comforting. I needed her to come more than I wanted to admit. Deep down, I knew the feeling was mutual. Elise, Spittle, and I planned to meet the next morning to map our routes. It had been a long while sense any of us in camp had set foot near 11D's rail yard. Between the three of us, no one had gone before. We couldn't leave much to chance.

This sort of anticipation never amounted to good things.

I flew a mission on a night similar to this. Only, there was no psithurism there. The sound of trees was replaced with helicopter propellers. The landing pad at a forward operating base outside of Iraq was pitch black. We proceeded like ants toward the tail to load up. Instructed with only hand gestures, we did as we were told. In my naïveté I believed it to be a cool experience. I was quickly humbled by the frigid demeanor of a young man, no older than twenty, with weapons strapped to his leg, chest, and sling. His moves were calculated. Buckling us each in. Testing our headsets. Easing the rear door up, locking it in at a forty-degree angle. Then steadying on bended knee glaring down the sights of a M4, he remained statuesque and motionless from that point on. My heartbeat in my ears, thoughts flowed rhythmically from one worst case scenario to the next. Looking at the other six faces I could tell they felt it too. It was eerie flying past the shadows of mountains, knowing what chaos occurred just beyond them. Looking at our gunny, he knew firsthand exactly where danger crept and what shape it took.

Five of the seven passengers had the same home station and worked together daily. Master Sergeant Traylor, the most senior of us all, sat across from me. It was his first overseas deployment. It was my third. He, along with two of my peers, were unfamiliar with that dull ache that crept into their chest. Being a part of a combat communications unit for all five years of my career, I was well acquainted with hazard zones and the fear that greeted you upon arrival.

"You good, Fisch?" I leaned away from my mic.

"Yeah, just trying to get my balls back down to where they belong," Fischer egged. It was good to know he was well enough to be sarcastic. Fischer was the youngest of us all. A fresh eighteen… and it showed. He either has a serious question or a smart-ass answer most of the time, but I enjoyed his demeanor. "How long before we touch down?" he asked.

"Who cares," Gonzales inserted. "This is cool."

"Gonzo, Goldfish, both of you shut up," Traylor piped in. That settled all dialogue instantly.

A few minutes later we had arrived. The air was dry and the landing pad dark. Once again we followed each other into one general direction before getting close enough to see our welcoming party.

"Welcome to paradise boys and girls!"

Freya stood confidently on the edge of the pad. Behind her were nameless faces shuffling our baggage from aircraft to flatbeds. "My name is Lt. Freya Nazzinin, you can call me LT, Naz, or Freya. Out here it's pretty lax." She turned to walk around some barricades that hid a bustling tent city. We said nothing and followed. "You are now at Joint Forces Camp Taybin. Officially, you are not here. All of your official paperwork including whatever medals you may earn while here will name Germany as your location. Do not take identifiable photos on or around camp and do not cupcake with your lovers at night and disclose your location. We have intel indicating some of our communications have been intercepted or attempted to be intercepted. With that said, after chow we have a meeting in our work trailer about setting up secure Wi-Fi and private networks for your laptops, smartphones, and thingamajigs."

She turned around taking small steps backwards like a flight attendant. "Here on your right is the gym. It is not a wellness club but has all the essentials. Across the gravel is the yard, for all my CrossFit junkies. It has everything you need for a good calisthenic workout."

Looking at both facilities, it was the most minimal experience I have had yet. The gym was a tin shed and the yard was an asphalt pad with a tarp overhang. "Males, you'll sleep here." She gestured towards a few tents past the yard. "And females, your tents are those three over there."

Continuing the tour we went into the morale, welfare, and readiness trailer to set eyes on our rec room. MWRs were a blessing in passing time out here. The latrine trailers occupied an entire aisle of the camp lot; separated with toilets and sinks in some, showers and sinks in others. Converted shipping containers and domed tents were most of the landmarks throughout our tour.

"Alright, these two tents serve chow three times a day and have a grab and go from lunch until midnight. You can sit in and eat here or the two tents directly across have extra seating. DO NOT eat in your sleep tents. We do have rats on camp and they'll eat through your clothes and bed sheets to find any crumbs you leave. Also, it is cool out now, but come spring, the snakes will be back. If you have rats you will have snakes so it's best to avoid the domino effect. You've been warned."

Typically encounters with brass were either abrasive or chill. Freya was a great mix of both. She was the most personably smug women I've met and I respected her instantly. "LT, where do we get linen?" I hesitated to ask.

"Great question," she said without a glance. She directed her answer to the crowd. "After you eat, when we meet up for debrief, I need all the senior leaders of each shop to give me a headcount. If I remember correctly, we have airfield comm, firefighter, power production, and civil engineering inbound, correct?" Her number two, a staff sergeant, nodded. "Okay great, airfield," she looked to MSgt Traylor. "I have your numbers."

MSgt Traylor rumbled a "HUA" in response, as in: heard, understood, acknowledged.

Freya continued, "I am a radio troop by trade but they've got me pushing paper this tour. So, I'll be handling your teams admin and intake. Everyone else, give me a good head count once you know. I suggest not over inflating numbers because you have nowhere to store extra blankets and it's hell trying to wash it all." The firefighters echoed an indicative laugh. "Well, I'll be in the office, I've already eaten dinner, when you guys are finished, head on over,"

"Will do Naz!" Fischer said oddly loud and embarrassingly eager. Gonzo slapped the back of Fischer's freshly-shorn head, putting an action to all of our thoughts. I could only shake my head at him as he walked in front of me to enter the chow tent.

"What is wrong with you?" I laughed. Fischer smirked and shrugged, turning redder by the second.

That was the first meal we had at Camp Taybin, and would be the same every Wednesday for the next thirty and a half weeks.

The first month was a blur of finding the best times to shower, eat, and do laundry. Trying to avoid the crowds and do the time with my head down, I didn't make too many acquaintances other than a few firefighters and Freya.

For the most part, our shop made our own schedules. Airfield was there as maintainers. As long as landing systems and navigational aids were working, we didn't have much to do. We would radio into air traffic control throughout the day to ensure everything was going well. Then, held routine maintenance bi-monthly to calibrate some of our equipment. The deployment was more of a mental game. Idle time needed to be filled with productivity. Freya had that part figured out. Most times I found her parked on a cinderblock bench reading a book. Or in the phone trailer cubicles, reading a book. Or behind her office desk, reading a book.

Around Christmas, the packages and cards started rolling in. Most of what Freya received was from patriots back stateside thanking her for her service. We all received similar sentiments, but mostly between the cards and care packages we got from relatives. It became evident that she didn't have those ties to back home. "My mom baked cookies and labeled each box for everyone, here is yours," I said handing her the wrapped gift.

Her face lit up, "Thank you, Nix."

I smiled. "Also, my sister made this." I pulled out a gingerbread house with little green army figurines glued around its perimeter. She stared at it and laughed.

"Aw, this is so sweet, how old is she?"

"Nineteen." I said, flatly. Freya covered her mouth laughing harder. "She's in school to become an architect. Well, civil engineering at Spellman. Then she'll go into architecture. She's always building something and thought this was funny. We usually have a gingerbread house building contest in my family around the holidays. Of course, she always wins." My mind drifted to her showing me around campus last time I came back from deployment.

"That's nice," Freya commented.

"What is?" I was confused by her statement.

"It's nice that your family has holiday traditions. Especially ones that surpass distance and borders."

Her words meant a lot, mainly because she was right. I deflected, "Are you and your family close?"

She looked me in the eye, "No, my family are my dogs and they're with a co-worker back in my shop if that answers your question." I was intrigued at how honest she was. But more curious as to why it didn't seem to affect her.

I cleared my throat. "LT, we're going to watch some movies in our work tent and drink a few beers, if you're interested."

"Nah," she didn't stall to respond, "I got something better than beer," she said lifting a bottle of Canadian whiskey.

We exited the office and walked almost entirely in silence. We mazed through camp and walked outside the barricade. Freya radioed into security forces and

ATC that we were approaching and crossing the flight line. After giving us the go ahead, we spoke again.

"You don't come out here often do you?" I teased. Her head was on a swivel trying to slice through the night surrounding us.

Freya glared at me. "Sure I have, during the day. It's not the most secure place on camp. Especially at night and you guys really hang out at work, after your shift, *willingly?*"

"Weren't you at your desk after hours? Plus, we're plenty safe out here. We've got that barbed wire protecting us." I said pointing a few yards out to the perimeter. We shared subdued chuckles.

"Oh yea, I feel incredibly safe. I'll just rely on boomer," she said, hand on her thigh holster.

"You know you aren't required to carry that?" I said.

"Well, I'll be sure to time how long it takes you to run to your bunk to get your M4, verses how long it takes me to draw my weapon and pull the trigger. You know, if we are ever under attack."

Touché.

We spent seven long months out there. Freya and I shared a few meals throughout that time too. We talked about our careers, places we've seen and wanted to go. I bored her with my summer camp stories of Elise and my youth. Explaining how I learned to rough it before military deployments. She humored me by listening and asking questions. I appreciated her friendship.

Walking into the admin trailer that April, she smiled a wide grin. "Nix, guess what?" I tilted my head curiously. She gushed, "We're all going home. The new team arrives in one week. We'll do a week or so turnover, then we'll be packing up."

I didn't need to hear any more. "I'll go tell the team."

We didn't waste any time. My shop got a head start on packing all non-essentials. Freya began the logistic planning for flights, cargo, and funding for our travel expenses. By the time the new team arrived we all had one foot out the door.

MSgt Traylor, TSgt Lile, myself, Gonzo, and Fisch all stood on the tarmac as the Helios turned off their engines. A familiar scene of trailing ants pooled in front of Freya. She welcomed them as we began tossing their bags to help deliver them to their tents. It was odd being on the other side of a scenario we all once lived through but, nonetheless, I was grateful it was over. We shook hands and made small talk as we walked part of the tour. Lile and Traylor arranged for some radio turnover the following day with the new leads. All while managing to eye the new females and creepily trail behind the group.

The next day after lunch, Lile stopped me. "Hey, Strachan, hold up. Can you take the evening shift and I'll be on call now till four for you? I didn't get any sleep last night and the sooner I get my shift over with the sooner I can go to bed."

"Sure man. Now I can go workout before the firefighters get off. Thanks," I said.

I went to my tent to begin changing when I realized my headphones were at the work site from the evening before. I spent most of my shift on the couch streaming movies or playing video games. Walking outside the barricade, I asked the watchmen to radio the tower and ask for permission to cross. Hearing the static response of "all clear" I walked towards the flight line.

One of our white pickups was parked adjacent to the control tower and technician tent. Initially, I dismissed its presence because of the traffic controllers I presumed to be on duty. That was until I saw another vehicle parked by the back tower door. Walking upward towards the hilltop site, I heard a familiar voice yell, "What the hell are you doing!?"

I broke into a sprint, unzipping the tent door I was stilled in what I saw. "LT, what's going on, are you alright?" My words raced. One of the new guys, was floundering on the couch holding his neck.

Winded, Freya said, "I'm fine, maybe you should ask this dipshit why his lips fell on my face and his hand on my ass." She shrugged, "So, my fist fell into his Adam's apple."

Before I knew what I was doing, I wrapped my hand around his throat to lift him to his feet. "What's up, *what's up!*" Is all my rage allowed me to repeat.

Freya saved him. "No, Nix, let him go," she said, unconvincingly.

"When you gather yourself," she looked in his direction. "Meet me in the command section so we can reunite you with a seventeen-hour plane ride." She walked out, I followed.

"What were you doing up here with that guy?" I asked. She stopped and stared me down. "I mean, I'm not blaming you but just curious. You're usually in the office this time of day."

She got into a stride again, "It was suggested I help spin the new folks up on how we do encrypted communications out here. Being that it's my trade, Lile asked me to give him some supplemental radio training for turnover. When I got here, he was the only one."

Anger instantly consumed me. *Lile orchestrated this.* I thought. Walking back into camp, Freya talked most of the way but I heard nothing. I was consumed in thought. Walking into the office trailer, there he was, standing over the new girl's shoulder, as she navigated the computer screen. They were mostly alone with the exception of Gonzo and some other guy. It didn't matter to me either way.

I rubbed my eyes to focus the anger, "Hey man, can I talk to you?" I said gesturing Lile to the door.

"Na, I'm busy, can we talk later?" he asked.

I charged his direction and grabbed the back of his shirt. "Nope, now," I demanded.

Ignoring his angry protest and the attempts Gonzo made to calm me, I threw Lile out the trailer. There stood Freya, and it seemed Lile had come to a conclusion of what this talk would be about.

"Tell me something, before I lose it. Why did you ask to take my shift, and I find you here? But before you do, why the fuck," my voice grew in tone. Did you ask LT to do radio turnover?"

He paused to search our faces. "Look last night the new guy was asking about some of the girls on camp and I asked about the newbies. He said he had a thing going with one but I could have her if I set him up with her." gesturing to Freya. I took a step forward. Gonzo read the moment and mustered his strength to catch my swing before it landed.

Freya inserted, collected and poised, "Well good, then you can join your buddy." Lile looked confused. "Fifteen-thirty in the command section, don't be late." Freya walked off.

"What the hell?" Lile questioned in her absence. "What the hell?" He then directed towards me.

"Yea, what the hell TSgt?" I said from behind Gonzales' bear hug. "You tried to pimp out our own. Piece of shit!"

Word spread fast about Freya being assaulted. It sent a shock wave at how fast command got the perps out of there. They had Freya's back and I did too. We only had a week left, but I knew she was glad not having to see either of them in camp. It put a damper on what was otherwise an alright deployment. Those last few days, I felt overly protective of Freya and the gossip that surrounded her incident. However, she kept her distance from me and the team. Only speaking to us about logistics of our departure. Being together seemed less likely after that. I hated that our friendship wasn't the same but respected her choice to shield her peace. Allowing her that was more important than sharing my love for her.

Our bases were both in Georgia but hours apart. The distance was most definitely felt. A year after our return, I emailed her that I was getting out and that rekindled a long-dead dialogue. I updated her on Lile's career decline from demotion to forced separation. As well as, the discharge process I was embarking on. She had sense reached out to her dad and some cousins, even planning a vacation with some. I was proud to have my friend back. We became friends on social media which made it easier to communicate. When the conflict began to boil over and random attacks on the street grew more common, I feared for her. The last thing I wrote was "get to somewhere safe."

She did.

FIVE

I WOKE UP TO A tempo I wasn't familiar with as a civilian. I woke at my normal time, and camp was bustling in motion. Two days had passed in what felt like a daze. We've been getting organized the last few days but seemed to hit a stride today. The kids were huddled over tubs, washing their own laundry. The elders chopped and sorted vegetables in a nearby garden. The adults were scattered about, gathering wood, setting lines and traps. Since the reserve was established, everyone has done their part, but tasks were completed leisurely throughout our days. Now, getting our chores out of the way early allowed for more time to train. More time to prepare.

Elise was already out of the cabin this morning which was unusual for her. After washing up and changing my shirt, I meander outside to find everyone. Walking into the dining facility, I saw Kayson and a few others putting empty trays away. It was rare that I was a part of the late crowd for breakfast but I appreciated the peace to gather my thoughts. Grabbing a bowl and spoon, I scooped my own oatmeal, and took a seat.

"Hey man, thought you might like some of these. I had some in the back." Kayson said cupping a hand of mixed berries.

"Wow, thanks Sonny." I was grateful but barely managed to sound enthused.

"Are you ready for today?" Kayson asked. "Have you checked the vehicles, your ammunition, what route you're taking?"

"We have, just got to get my head in the game." I said, Sonny nodded. He placed his hand on my back before giving me a firm pat.

"Well, alright then, I'll leave you to it." His words drifted as he walked off.

I fished into my bag, for loose ammo, and began combining them into their designated box. Then filling every magazine I had. Rifle bullets were hard to come by, but we snagged cases from local reserve armories and pawn shops before things got bad. Luckily we never had to use much of it. The way folks panic purchased a few months ago reminded me of hurricane season or the pandemics of years past. However, this paradigm, this time around, seemed to have more merit.

Within the hour we would be en route to the rail yard. Spittle and Elise, for the most part, took the lead in logistics. Lamor helped them with planning and spun them up on their field care in case one of us gets hurt or injured. Elise cleaned our guns and sharpened knives the night before. I organized our packs with Freya to ensure we each had first aid, ammo, and signals on our person. I checked every box over and over again. Until the clink of my spoon at the bottom of my bowl punctuated the mental checklist. We were as prepared as we were going to be. I needed to find Spittle and Elise to hear them echo the same sentiment.

I found them both at Freya's cabin. "Mornin' Nix." Freya initiated.

"Morning. Good morning everybody," I said.

Spittle lifted his head, gaging my posture. "You ready buddy. If we leave within the hour we can make it to the outpost by noon." We agreed that we would drive to the pitstop and leave the vehicle as a decoy. From there we would walk on foot to the outpost. That would give us time to rest, have a bite to eat and prepare to trek to the next checkpoint where we stored another vehicle. If we were being surveilled, our methods would disorient them. While we needed to get to 11D urgently, we couldn't risk camp exposure going directly from point A to point B.

"Yea Spit, I'm good to go man. What you got there?" I changed the subject. Freya loved that I asked.

"I fabricated the shell of this boombox to optimize usability and speaker clarity. It functions the same as a stereo would, except its inner parts are advanced analog and can tune into the higher frequencies that these handhelds function on. This one is yours." Her expertise on the subject matter made us all beam. She continued. "This is the other radio you'll be delivering to 11D. It's a 1319 transceiver. It can receive and transmit on any in-range frequency. Small, effective, and durable. We have another here that I have some calibrating left to do. I'll be able to hear you if you key the frequency but I won't be able to respond just yet. A problem I hope to have fixed before you all head back this way. Unfortunately though, once you guys do embark on your return you'll have no way of talking to us on this thing." She placed a hand on the boom box, "Only listening in. So be fast and be safe." She gazed around the room so we each could feel her intensity. We shook our heads *yes* in compliance. Isaac walked in with a pack strapped to his back.

"Hey, Mi amigas and amigos." He bowed slightly.

"What's up man?" I asked gesturing to his bag.

"I'm tagging along. And before you start, Angelique is good with it." His words rushed to cut me off. "The way I see it. If you all die before delivering the radio or getting good intel what use is that for my family or the reserve. You got 9 and 3 from what I see. You still need someone to cover your 6. I'm going."

"Woo, It's a party now." Spittle jived into a little dance. His futile attempts to break tension was one of his best and worst characteristics.

"Alright man, let's do it," I said. Giving each other a backhanded pound, we confirmed a united front.

Isaac has been my best friend for eight years. We went from being neighbors to being brothers. We didn't always agree but could always put our differences in perspective.

"Alright little badger scouts, are we ready?" Elise urged.

"Let's do it." My words fell out.

A few onlookers stood and watched as we disappeared into the brush. The sound of our footsteps synced, cracking twigs beneath them. We moved quickly starting with Isaac as our point. Spittle wasn't a regular on these treks but surely held his own. He and I had somewhat of a history with the short time spent down range, but nothing remarkable. My trust for him was merely an extension of Freya's voucher.

Reaching the vehicles camouflaged in brush, we each began uncovering the SUV. "Shotgun," Spittle cackled. Each set of eyes became blades, slashing through Spit's face.

Once we got inside, Elise unhinged, "For the duration of this mission I'm going to need you to shut the fu—"

"Whoa mama, I didn't know y'all had assigned seats," he joked.

Elise had a low threshold for bullshit. Unfortunately, Spittle seemed to have an endless supply of it.

"El, be cool," I requested.

"I'm cool, but *he* will not be the reason—"

"*He* has feelings," Spittle injected. "—alright, *alright* y'all. Look, I crack jokes. Too many jokes. My bad, but this shit is stressful."

Shadows of a smirk traced our faces. I understood if that's how he coped. You had to respect his willingness to explore humor even if it's at the worst time.

Before any of us knew it, Elise navigated us to the back of the pit stop.

We all hopped out and moved diligently towards the rear entrance. Once inside, after scanning the room, Isaac pushed over a postcard stand to startle any potentially hidden threats. We frequented this rest stop enough to know if someone were present and where they'd be hiding if they were. I walked behind the counter to pick up the paper. *No new thread,* I thought.

I had hoped there would be a new transmission so we no longer needed to take this course. Most of the aisles had been looted leaving sparse items throughout the store. Elise came from the back room with Spittle following.

"Y'all ready to head out?" Spit inquired. "I'm good if y'all are."

"Yeah let's go," I said.

Elise tied her hair up away from her face. She directed her words to Spittle intently. "We're going to head across the street to that tree line over there. Move quick and stay low. Do not ask questions. Do not make small talk. The house is about three and half hours out on foot. Stop when we stop. Go when we go."

"I've got a question, when do I get to pee ma'am?" Spittle teased.

Elise's eyes rolled like dice in her head.

I attempted to offset their bickering, "Spit, I'll run point, just follow up on me like combat training. Isaac will pick up the rear."

"What use to be Georgia SWATS' finest baby." Isaac announced, arms wide and proud. I laughed understanding his pride in service.

"Let's go," I refocused.

Leaning into the door, my body pressed against the glass, looking onto the buildings peripheral spaces.

We exited swiftly with a steady pace. On our way to the tree line our cadence quickened. A combination of nerves and survival were swimming upstream in a flood of adrenaline. Going along like that for a while, we made good time. Halfway into the trek we stopped to rest near a nondescript tree. All of us pulled out water bottles to coat our dry throats and wash sweat from our faces. I couldn't help but think about camp. Especially Freya. I looked up and Elise was sharpening her knife. Spit seemed to be sharpening his tongue, silently laughing at his own jokes. Isaac was reading a map with his usual serious expression. The suns off-centered position let us know we had a few hours left of sunlight.

"I'll be back," Elise notified us.

"I gotta take a leak," Spittle said shortly after her departure.

"Where did you think she was going?" I asked humorously. Spittle's head tilted in his delay of understanding, before turning around to walk away himself. The forest was silent except the near distant sound of him urinating. We waited.

* * *

Inhale, exhale, I calculated each breath to keep endurance. My eyes scanned left and right, never looking down to maintain my footing. We were almost there. And while there was no present day feeling of safety, having four walls around you at least provided the false illusion.

Spittle closed the distance between us and gave my shoulder a firm squeeze to halt my steps. I raised my right fist to signal the others trailing behind. We all stopped. Our intervals closed and he reached his hand into my eyeline gesturing to the far right. There was movement.

We all laid prone, stomachs parallel to the dirt. We stared down our sights in our respective directions. Readying ourselves, index fingers floating over the trigger. Before another thought could complete, a shot rang out. Followed by a loud thud. Isaac and Elise turned startled, trying to see what just happened. Spittle sprung to his feet. Slinging his rifle and pulling a firearm in one fluid motion. Guns aimed at an unknown threat we each followed. Spittle dove into a light brush grabbing the carcass by the ankles. "Winner, winner, vulture dinner."

We all dropped our weapons. Reading our faces, he quickly blurted, "I didn't know it was an animal when I shot it. But I'm glad I did. Dark meat or white meat?" He smiled at Elise.

"Dark," she said. "But, we gotta get out of here. Who knows who heard that shot?"

She was right. Without another word, we helped Spittle sling up the bird and we started off. *Inhale, exhale, control your breathing* replayed in my mind. Being out of the service and out of shape, my body was no longer conditioned for this type of movement. We just needed to make it to the house.

* * *

The back side of the development was marked with overturned clay. These woods were dug up and used to fill foundations and give the big houses bigger hills to judge from atop of. We made good time. The closer we grew to our beloved outpost the more I could taste my favorite cup of dry noodles.

Excitement was short-lived once we saw an unfamiliar vehicle parked up the street. Was it abandoned? Could it be trouble? I signaled towards it, and immediately Elise and Isaac branched off. I whispered near to Spittle. "We've got company." He nodded and we all surrounded the neighboring homes. Scanning our safe haven first, we then moved on to the other three homes in this under-developed cul-de-sac. Scanning windows, back and front yards—we saw and found no one.

"Clear."

"Clear," we all echoed as reassurance. Our guards were let down in that moment.

"Welp, is it lunch time?" Spittle laughed but appeared serious.

Spittle had never been to the outpost but quickly made himself at home. Upon entry, Isaac gave him the lay of the land. "There's water in the basement and some canned goods. Amo is in the pantry. The plumbing doesn't work but there's plenty landscape outside and some TP to wipe. If something's up, whistle twice."

"Got it," Spittle assured. "Where's the cookies?"

We all splintered taking the few seconds of solitude the moment offered us.

Walking down into the basement for a pre-nap snack, I found Isaac grabbing some water. Exhaustion filtered over both of our faces. We shared no words, just gestures of food offering.

I passed Spittle on the couch on my way upstairs where all curtains were pulled closed, leaving a remnant effect of prewar existence, with an emptiness of long abandoned life. Overly fortified shelter indicated inhabitants. We secured our location through hidden riggings and interior boarding.

Elise stood statuesque in the master bedroom. Adjacent to the window and just out of sight, she stood watch.

"Did you eat?" I asked, throwing canned meat on the bed.

"No, I'm good, breakfast is holding me over." Her gaze never dropped.

"I'll take over. You've been up here almost an hour. You should rest," I offered. She was silent. "It's cool, El. Isaac is downstairs, and Spittle is with him. Sleep while you can." I nodded towards the bed.

She took her pistol out of her waistband and laid flat on her back. After a few slight shifts, with her hands folded over her chest, I could hear her breath deepen. My eyes held a slight weight, but I physically shook it off. Sitting there I couldn't help but let my mind drift. I thought of our parents, where they could be. The holidays that were soon approaching and my other siblings. Torturous memories of our siblings and how much I missed them, film reeled in my thoughts.

The world went black as my lids closed.

SIX

NO TIME HAD PASSED BEFORE a distant static eased my eyes back open. There was a tone, a pause, then another. I inhaled deeply, waking myself more vigorously, then listened again. A tone, a pause, then a tone surrounded by static. *Is that the reserve?* I couldn't comprehend what I was hearing until instinct took over. "Wake up, wake up!" I shouted to Elise springing out the door and down the stairs. "Isaac," I called out.

"Yo," he answered.

"Where's Spit?" I looked to the couch.

"He went out to take a leak and gather wood to cook the bird," Isaac said confused by my panic.

"Fuck!" I couldn't hold back.

I dressed with gear as I headed to the back. "The whistle. I heard him whistle through the radio."

Weapons in hand, we spilled out the back door.

I could see him maybe 100 yards out fixed with his rifle poised. Every breath made my throat dryer. My pace quickened, but I couldn't reach him fast enough.

At our feet laid a woman. We stood staring at Spittle and back at her, trying to wrap our minds around what occurred.

"I tried to whistle when she was further off but then she saw me. She took off—I ran her down and knocked her out. Not sure where she was *running to* though," Spittle confessed.

"Who. *Who* she was running to." I turned around scanning the subdivision. "Let's grab her and bring her to the basement. Find out why she's here and who's with her." Isaac and I scooped her up to bring her inside before anyone else could spot us. Spittle was visibly freaked out once we got inside and Elise kept peering out of the window.

"Tie her up in the basement. Isaac and I will do another sweep." I said.

"Nah man, I'll go, it's my mess." Spit's southern drawl bound each word.

I nodded. "Show me where you saw her and which direction she ran." As we headed towards the backyard Isaac and Elise continued tying the woman up.

"How old do you think she is?" Elise inquired of Isaac as she brushed her blonde hair out of her face.

Isaac leveled himself to be eye-to-eye with the woman. "Maybe, twenty-five-ish? She looks awfully young."

* * *

Spittle and I continued into the backyards of each home. Starting at the first home at the top of the street, we worked our way inward down to the cul-de-sac. House after house we cleared until we got to the sixth home. "Let's head back." I said nonchalantly.

"No man, we can flush them out," Spittle said confidently.

I agreed, but I continued, "We could, but why waste our efforts. We have a long way to go to 11D." I started walking back.

Confused and still defiant Spit replied, "I guess." Then followed me back.

When entering the outpost Spittle and I headed straight to the basement. When I noticed the young woman coming back to, I initiated with, "We found 'em." Everyone's eyes got big including Spittle's. The woman's face screwed, shaking her head. I waved them into the hall out of eyesight. As I spoke, I began hand signaling the opposite. "Yup we found 'em at the other house." I shook my head slowly and deliberately and pointed through the wall at our captive. I grabbed my ears and pointed back to the room.

Elise gave me an exaggerated wink. "Great, what do you want to do with them?" The other's expressions adjusted confirming their understanding.

"I say we question them separately, they give good intel, great. If not, we get rid of them," Isaac said.

We all coordinated and walked back into the room, she was fully conscious.

Spittle jumped right in. "Do you remember me, honey?"

She glared, seething at him.

Elise casually leaned against a cabinet. "What's your name?"

The woman shook her head in resistance.

"Listen," I said. "You can tell us or we can ask your Scourge friend." Her eyes daggered through me.

"What is your name?" Elise stated more sternly.

"Charlotte," she spoke to the floor.

"What are you doing out here, Charlotte?" Elise pressed. "Who is that you were running to? Friend? Family? Scourge buddy?"

Charlotte's emotions swirled into a look, exhibiting fear turned confusion. "*You* aren't

Scourge?" she asked. She jumped from face-to-face waiting for nonverbal confirmation.

Isaac stomped towards her aggressively checking her pockets, waistband, and socks. He looked up while on one knee and slowly swayed his head left to right. "Nothing," he said.

"Charlotte, I'm losing patience. You aren't an ally so *who* are you?" My tone was sharp.

"And who is that in the other room?" Elise added.

"That's my—my mom. I was gathering food when I saw him. I thought he was Scourge and I was going to go warn her," Charlotte finally admitted.

"What's your cause?" Elise pried, eyebrow raised. The silence that followed Elise's question left the room unconvinced.

Isaac and Spittle removed their knives from their holsters. "I think she's Scourge, guys," Isaac said disappointed.

"No, no, no." Charlotte tensed up. "No, not anymore!" We all stopped. Elise and I looked at each other.

Head tilted, El gained more traction and followed up. "Explain!"

"I, we, were a part of it. We lived there and we escaped," Charlotte said.

"Aw you were held hostage?" Spittle mocked without sympathy.

"No. We—at first, we were there because we wanted to be. We thought it was right. But, then, more and more people were being *selected*. They make it sound good but it's bullshit. More people weren't meeting the 'standard.' They asked my parents to do *something,* but they declined. Then they decided my mom would be the community sacrifice to show our commitment to God. My dad freaked and that night planned our escape. We ran until we found this place." Charlotte's eyes never left the ground as she told us her story. "We've never hurt anyone." She finally looked us in the eye. "We were Scourge because we didn't want our country to go to shit, we didn't want our society to crumble from people doing whatever."

"Bang-up job, honey," Spittle said plainly.

"Our," Elise repeated silently. "Our."

Looking in her direction, Charlotte was confused.

"*Our country, our society.* That 'our' includes us. " Elise said walking towards the door. "I'll be sure to grab a mirror on the way back so you can see who's causing the crumble."

Elise made an impact upon her exit as she always does. Sadly, I believed Charlotte. I was dumbfounded and disinterested at this point. "Untie her," I said. "She's useless to us." I started out and up the stairs.

"What about my mom?" Charlotte asked. Spittle began cutting the ties around her ankles.

"Go find her," he answered.

Charlotte's stutter ensued. "I thought, I thought you…"

"We lied," Isaac responded bluntly.

As I moved towards the basement door from the main level, I nodded at Elise who was standing in the hall. I walked back in holding the carcass in a bag. "Here. You look like you need food." I dropped the bag at her feet. "If you and your mom come after us, I will kill you. If you *send* someone after us, we will kill them, then I will kill you." The room hung on my every word. "Eat this, get your strength and leave. Do not come back."

Charlotte remained silent. She slowly picked up the bag now that she was free. Every few steps, she looked back at us confirming we made no sudden moves. I called out to Elise for Charlotte's own safety. "El, she's coming up." We slowly followed. Once we all resurfaced Elise's eyes were glued to Charlotte. El never blinked. Charlotte cracked the front door and slid out of it facing us the entire time.

We all stared at the door when Isaac broke the silence. "We should go." He was right.

"Let's grab some water and go as soon as the sun sets. We'll stay in the trees and follow the road." Elise then asked the obvious. "Do you think they'll come for us?"

"No. I think they're willingness to stay alive supersedes their hate for us," I said.

"Finally," Elise said, almost smiling.

We spent the next several minutes gathering more supplies. We had an hour or so until dark, but our packs were ready to go. Spittle offered to keep watch so the rest of us could take a power nap and recharge. It may have been offered out of guilt but I was ready to oblige. I laid there on the couch until the silence grew more silent. My limbs became relaxed and the grip on my gun loosened. It was only a few moments before I found rest and REM sleep met me with open arms. I was out.

Before I knew it, an hour had past and the room I opened my eyes to had a blue-ish tint. I looked up to see Spit still sitting at the window. Hearing the rustling of my movement behind him, he looked over. "Welcome back, bud."

I yawned obnoxiously. Still looking around.

"Elise is in that bedroom," Spit said pointing to an adjacent room. "And Isaac is somewhere upstairs." I only managed to nod as I got my bearings. I walked to the window near him and peeked out. I saw smoke rising from up the street and immediately knew its indication. Spittle and I looked at each other and he offered a wry look.

"There will be more birds. Better birds," I said dismissing it. "I'll go wake everyone."

I wanted Elise to get as much rest as possible, so I headed upstairs. In the third room I found Isaac already awake. "What's up bruh?" He gave me a pound. "Do you see this?" he pulled the curtain back.

"Yeah, I saw." I said.

"Spit's pissed huh?" Isaac laughed. We shared in the amusement.

"Heading out in ten, man." I walked back out. Going downstairs the emptiness in my stomach became apparent. I grabbed the peanut butter I left on the counter and started in. "Hey El." I walked into the bedroom. Immediately she jumped up. I knew better than to leave that statement unfinished. "Everything is fine. It's time to get up, we leave in ten." She calmed herself, nodded, and wiped her eyes. I came back into the living room as Isaac met me and Spit.

"Good to go, man?" Isaac asked Spittle.

"Yep," Spit said.

At that moment I felt my heartbeat quicken. The ability for your body to go into survival mode is interesting. Occurrences, or even scents and sounds are enough to let your body know it is in danger and needs to preserve itself. At this moment, we were in danger. I made a dash for the stairs to investigate. Spit went back to the window yet saw nothing. Isaac came rushing behind me to look out from the front bedroom. We looked out each window until we had the best vantage point. Engines. Truck engines roared at varying pitches as they weaved up and down the hilly main road.

Without words we both rushed downstairs. Elise and Spittle were already at the backdoor.

"That freaking bi—" Spittle started.

"Listen, we run to that runoff ditch behind the houses. When they go into the house, we take off for the trees." Everyone nodded.

We opened the backdoor guns drawn and could hear the engines getting louder as they approached.

"Go," Isaac whispered and we all went into full-sprint. Laying in the ditch, we could see the glare of their headlights as they turned into the cul-de-sac.

"Let's go." I said. We stayed low and moved fast. Until we heard the engines lull. They stopped. We dropped to our stomachs again and aimed the guns between the houses. *They're coming,* I thought.

Then I heard a shrill scream. My finger hugged the trigger waiting, in anticipation.

"No!" I heard an agonized screech. *Bang!* The power of the weapons round echoed, bouncing off the walls of the subdivision. "NO!" The voice screamed again. Charlotte threw her weight to the ground as a group tried to pick her up, dragging her out of the house. Another woman was slung over the shoulder of a large man as he walked to the SUV throwing it inside. "Let me go! Pleaseee!" Charlotte begged. She flung herself this way and that trying to escape. I could only see a little of her in the gaggle. She kept trying to run in the direction of our hideout, only meeting resistance. Her pleas became muffled when they finally shoved her into the second vehicle. With their desired cargo secured, the three trucks shifted into gear. They began driving off in the direction from which they came and the engines' sound faded into nothingness. My heartbeat slowed. We all rose to our feet in disbelief.

"We have to go," Isaac urged. Compliant, we started walking into the night. We had a long night ahead of us, but at this point, nothing could be more draining.

SEVEN

FINALLY WE FOUND THE OUTER railroad. We were close. In moments we all picked up our pace. Internally, I was running on fumes but I couldn't stop. Elise must have seen the pain in my face and the weight of my steps.

"We're almost there." She placed her hand on my upper back gently guiding me forward. Only a few more steps. I conditioned my mind. Breaking our trek up into small sections. If I make it to that tree. If I make it to that pinecone. My thoughts cycled creating small markers to make it more manageable. My vision blurred, bright spots showed ahead of me.

Isaac was unzipping my pack, jolting me back to. "Naz! Naz!" His rasp barely let the words escape. He keyed the radio, "Hey girl, it's good to hear your voice."

"Did you guys make it okay?" she asked through interference.

"We haven't made it to the rail yard yet. I'll explain later, but we'll call in when we do."

"Hello, can you hear me?" Freya begged.

"Yes I'm here, we're here." Isaac exclaimed.

"If you can hear me, I'm going to keep trying. Be safe." Freya affirmed.

Isaac put the radio into his bag. His disappointment couldn't be veiled behind his concern. "Buddy, you alright? Didn't you hear the radio?" Isaac asked.

"My bad man. I, my mind drifted." I couldn't tell him how weak I felt.

He just nodded accepting my omission.

"Weapons up!" Elise announced. We all began slinging our rifles and Spittle looked on unsure.

"Wha—" Spit started.

To which I pointed, "We're here."

The brush was wide-spanning with a maze of railroad tracks ahead of us going in every direction. Abandoned cargo trailers sat aloof. As we approached the rail yard center, the train connections became more concentrated.

11D was an intentional fortress of steel. The carts were positioned to funnel us inward to their main point of entry. When the civil war started, the transportation hub became abandoned. The 11D community saw that as an opportunity to take full advantage of. Train cars and shipping containers became border walls or insulated living quarters. The pathway narrowing, dark and unclear, we stopped at the sound of a weapon charging.

Our hands in the air Elise called out, "Allies!" A flashlight shown over the steel wall, passing over each of our faces. Elise pulled her sleeve down showing her green bandana. A series of unhinging, prelude to the door whipping opening. Silhouettes stood, staring at us down their barrel sites. No one said a word.

I cleared my throat. "We're from the Refuge. We've been communicating through paper threads at the—"

"What's your cause?" A voice inquired. A pause stilled the air until Spittle spoke.

"2 and 4," Spittle pained.

"2nd Amendment, 4th Amendment, 8th, and the 14th," Isaac became emboldened.

"2, 4, 8,13,14, and 15," I announced.

"Same!" Elise said bluntly. "Plus 19 and 26." Her voice sharpened with each word.

"Come with me," the voice instructed. The small crowd parted creating space for us to walk in, one behind the other, Elise first, unfazed by the lack of hospitality. We knew it was warranted, although, we are who we claim to be. As the small militia thinned, a man of medium build was left weaving ahead. Four armed men and women followed up the rear. Elise slowed as our group moved towards a dark void in the rail yard. We were circled, in front of us, a bordered dead end. "Come on." The bearded man turned to us revealing his face. He slid a door open on a trailer revealing rigged fireworks and explosives. We stalled. "It's fine." he said, urging continued movement. He hopped into the trailer and high-stepped around the ordinances. Reaching the far wall, he slid open a secret door. On the other side, a seemingly quaint tiny home park. Rows and rows of containers were lined up. Most doors left opened while the inhabitants rested. Once crossed over the barrier, we could see they were insulated and furnished. As we walked by, I was amazed. We all were.

Quietly, our ensemble of misfits moved pass the housing units to stacked shipping containers. An inconspicuous staircase brought us up to an old office unit. We all walked inside shocked to encounter electricity.

"Holy shit," Spits slurred. Isaac backhanded his arm.

"Welcome y'all." The bearded man turned to us. "I'm Anthony. Behind you is Josh, Amanda, Kenzie, and Duke. We all interchangeably shook hands.

"It's nice to meet you all," I bantered. "I'm Nixon."

"Elise," El inserted raising her hand. "That's Isaac and Spit." She pointed.

"Nice to meet ya'. But, what brings y'all here?" Anthony got right down to it.

"Look." Isaac scanned the room. "We got a message a week ago from you all at the gas station on old state road. It said to leave camp and we wanted to know why? What do you all know that we don't?"

The third silence of the night and it didn't feel good. "What!" I found myself demanding.

Josh chimed in from behind, walking around in front of us. "Um, that wasn't us."

His squad followed and we all faced each other. "The last message we left was over a month ago about some movement within the uncivil and the dialysis clinic. We never said anything about uprooting."

My stomach dropped immediately. What did he mean they never sent us a bulletin. If not them, who, and how?

"Wait," I said needing to process.

Elise finished my thought, "What do you mean you never sent us a message?"

I began pulling our past correspondence out of my bag. I walked over to a desk and all nine of us huddled around in observation. I tried to sequence them best I could from memory and thread numbers.

"I have most of our recents, too," Amanda said, as she laid their papers on the table.

"Look, here's the food drop, to the safe house," Josh said. "Then, the inventory you responded with after your drop."

Kenzie continued, "Here's the refugee movement we told y'all about moving through GA. Here's the fish you guys sent us and the canned goods we exchanged."

"Amo, no update, dialysis clinic, no update." Isaac listed off each thread.

"Then here, '7b has comm. Gear.'" I traced the words with my fingers. "'Relocate your group. Leave nothing behind,' right there." I said, insistently.

Anthony and Josh locked eyes and Josh shook his head. The others in their group echoed the motion. Anthony looked at me, not sure what words to say.

Isaac and Spittle began dropping their bags, settling into this new development.

"But no, it was good intel. It was accurate information. See," Elise said pointing to the radios that emerged from their packs.

Amanda hovered over the desk, closely analyzing the pages. "Look! We didn't write this." Her finger laid heavily on the page. "Whenever we started a conversation with you all, we circled the page number. Every time! New topics, we wrote the number one, AND circled the page numbers. We only underlined the page number as responses."

"What!?" Isaac said flustered. His response wasn't as much a question as it was an angry statement.

"That makes no sense" Elise said. "Who then, who would write to us and help us. Who would tell us where to find supplies and warn us?"

"Where did they go?" I blurted out. The room looked lost.

"The refugees, I assume they were allies? Where'd they go?" I questioned further.

"I'm not sure. They mentioned Tennessee, but I'm not sure." Anthony responded. "They couldn't have…" He stopped himself.

"They could have watched you all. Found out about the pitstop," I said.

"But why then help us and not you guys. They knew of you all and your camp, why not help you and warn you too?" Spittle said.

"Maybe they were." said Elise. She didn't dare drift from her train of thought by looking at any of us. She just stared indirectly, eyes glazed and continued, "You said yourself, that the only correspondence with an underlined page number and "1" written was initiated by us to you as a response. Maybe they knew that or maybe they didn't. What they did know is that you all sent and received messages from that pitstop. We just inadvertently intercepted it. Maybe it was for you." Her eyes got big as she just enlightened the group.

"Who were these refugees?" Isaac asked.

"A small family, mom, dad, and daughter I think." Josh said approaching Anthony, trying to rub the stress from his shoulders. "They weren't here long. Barely a day. The mother and daughter didn't say much. They were so distraught, like they had had enough of this unrest. Just in shock, poor things."

Elise, Spittle, Isaac, and I looked to each other for comfort. We couldn't sink more than we already had. I had hoped the answer to my next question would be the life raft we all desperately needed. "Was the daughter blonde, maybe, early twenties?" I asked thinking, Say no, say no.

Anthony responded, "Yeah she was, you know her?"

"Just met her," Spittle answered. "Her Scourge buddies just grabbed them up."

"What, when, what do you mean?" Amanda showed concern.

Isaac mustered. "They were at the outpost community. Said they were prior Scourge. On the run."

Anthony looked angry. "They never, we never knew that. We let them in!" His voice grew louder.

"That's probably why they warned you all. You showed them kindness. They probably didn't say anything out of fear of retaliation." I tried to console the room.

"Then why did they tell y'all." Josh demanded.

"Tying someone up and interrogating them tends to reveal some things," Spittle quipped. "We thought they were hunting us, but turned out they were on the run."

"You said family?" I asked of Anthony and Josh. "You said the refugees were a small family."

Elise said, "When we interrogated the girl, she only mentioned her mom. She said her dad stayed behind." The 11D members stared at us in disbelief.

"Where's the father?" Elise asked.

Stunned, no one moved.

SEVEN B

THE CAMP WAS QUIET AND calm for midday. The absence of children playing was replaced with Dani's distant voice providing instruction. After seeing the gang off, I tinkered in the cabin. Steam brushed my face as I soldered an exposed wire, connecting it to a metal conductor. "Damn it!" I yelped, pressing a burned fingertip into a damp cloth. Needing a break, I stood, and left the soldering iron on its coil to smolder.

Angelique approached, giving a light knock on the door casing. "Heya, Freya." She chuckled to herself. "Want to give me a hand? This weapons training is going to start soon and I can't exactly demonstrate shooting positions with this belly." She rubbed her stomach attentively.

"I would, but I'm so close with this radio. Would you mind asking Lamor?" I suggested.

A soft smile folded into her cheeks. "Sure, no worries." Angelique encouraged. "How's it coming?"

All I could muster was a head shake of defeat.

"You'll get it, you will. I'll be back later though, got to find Lamor before this training starts," she said on her way out.

"Sure, and thanks." I waved goodbye.

I stood to regain focus, and get my blood flowing. *I wonder how Nix is holding up?* My thoughts drifted. I buried my face in both hands. My fingers glided from my forehead through my scalp. I gripped at my hair roots hoping the pain would jolt my brain. *My frequency range isn't stable. Why? I can't steady the range without it jumping. Why?* I paced.

"Why isn't my output stable?" I grunted out loud.

Because my input isn't stable. I gasped. My adrenaline flooded in from the discovery. I can't get a stable frequency range because my input isn't stable. My input is the reference point. Inconsistency yields poor results, I thought that advice was only good for training. My dad was a smart man. I need a good reference frequency. I have to trace it back. Wow, I miss him. My thoughts zigged and zagged connecting memories and whims of emotion. Refusing to settle into those feelings, I pressed on. It had been years since I was this hands-on with something so complex. Being a military officer meant more meetings and paperwork than hands-on technician work. I missed it. I smiled to myself. I still got it.

Successfully soldering the wire and removing the oscillator component, I leaned back. This seemed as good a stopping point as any. Exuding accomplishment, I exited my cabin. Propping the screen door open with a rock, as I always do when I leave, I started the short walk towards the shore. I was used to seeing Isaac somewhere near the water but his usual place on the shoreline was vacant. Walking along the waterline, careful to not get wet, I started to pray.

Dear God, I come to you with my heart open and humbled. I am grateful for your presence in my life and the protection over it. Keep me Lord. Keep me encouraged. Keep me positive. I pray for those engulfed in hate, I pray they be filled with peace. I pray that we all receive insight and be enlightened by the truth of the word. Guide us Father God. We need you. Lord thank you for your grace and mercy. Thank you for your love and the presence of Spirit. In your name I'll continue to pray, Amen.

Calm washed over me. Along with the splashes of water from me drifting. If I couldn't meditate, I had to at least pray. I don't think I've ever had anxiety per se, but I know I've had an unsettled spirit. I've had internal unrest telling me when something just isn't right, for me. I relied on that, now more than ever. I couldn't allow this world to harden me. My purpose is greater than that. I couldn't allow it. I inhaled sharply and gathered my thoughts. Walking back towards camp I could smell fish cooking and became excited to see what Kayson had thrown together.

Kayson was steady at his usual station behind the wood stove. "Fish patties!" He showed a wide grin.

"Oooh," I responded enthusiastically.

He finished, "We didn't hoist our usual catch this morning so I grabbed some veggies from the garden and some flour and bread scraps. Almost anything I could find to stretch it out."

It smelled amazing. Then a few glasses caught my eye. "What is that?" I asked less pleased. The prep wasn't as glamorous as the final product.

"Oh, that's just fish oil." Seeing my confused expression he continued, "How else did you think I was frying things back here." We both laughed.

"But how did you…" I started to ask. "It smells great Sonny."

He smiled, handing me a plate with two patties. I took the plate with a smile to match his, understanding the oil was a secret he wouldn't reveal. I stood watching in awe. Not sure if this was Sonny's enjoyment or his own form of meditation. I quietly finished my servings and rinsed the plate in the bucket of water. Walking out of the dining hall I noticed Angelique, Lamor, and Dani had part of the camp gathered. I went nearer to see what was the commotion.

"Ready, set, go!" Dani egged the youth on.

The clinking of metal pieces began as the four kids quickly disassembled and began reassembling their weapons. The adults watched and cheered them on.

"Focus, girl you got this! Good job, Lynn, let's go!" Lamor showed his competitive support.

Three racks and a click, was the sound of Lynn charging her weapon to show accurate assembly. She pulled the charging handle back, hit the bolt paddle, manually locking her bolt chamber back. Showed the clear chamber and put her hands up signaling completion. The kids all laughed and Lynn received a few congratulatory pats on the back.

"Great job, everyone, great job!" Dani said proudly. "Y'all get a fifteen-minute break. Then we'll come back for one final parts list and function review." Dani managed the groans. "It'll be quick and then we'll break for lunch."

"Yes!" they harmonized before running off.

"I'll help you clean up after," Lynn offered with one arm around Dani. Dani's arm rested on her shoulders, she smiled down at Lynn and nodded. They gave each other a tight squeeze before Lynn went off to join her friends..

"You do so great with them Dani," I started warmly.

"Yeah, well," Dani said, country and coy. "How's those radios coming along?" she changed subjects.

"Don't ask," I said plainly.

"Well, let me know if you need a hand later. I broke a few GPS devices on a couple hunting trips. So, I know a little something about getting back from broke." Though odd, her offer was well-intentioned. I politely accepted and started to make my way back to my cabin.

The sun's position changed the lighting around camp. It was my favorite time of day. Hours had passed of productive troubleshooting and my brain was exhausted. I sat upright on my bed with my eyes pressed closed. I was so close, I just wanted to finish. I cracked my knuckles but before I could get up, the hairs on my arms stood.

"Ahhhhhh" A deep painful yell rang out. Running down my cabin steps I looked around camp. Everyone was still and searching for the source of alarm.

"Ahhhhhh" the yell echoed again. It was coming from the woods. I bolted back inside grabbing my gun from under the bed and tucked my knife into my boot. Moving through camp, I became synced with Lamor and Dani running in the same direction. Weapons drawn, we moved in closer to the cries of pain.

"This way." Dani directed. She seemed more knowledgeable than us. She was right. Dani walked us directly to a sprawling man on the ground. His leg partially mutilated by a well-placed bear trap. Though sympathetic, my aim never wavered.

"Who the hell are you?" I asked blankly.

"HELP ME! Please," he begged. Lamor scanned our surroundings, distrustful of the circumstance.

"*Who*, are you?" I demanded.

"My name is Stephen!" he grunted. "Stephen. Now please help me!"

"What are you doing here?" I inquired, ignoring his pain.

"Please!" he pleaded again. "Please get this thing off me."

Dani took slight pity and began unhinging the trap. Although, she could have afforded to be more gentle. Lamor helped pry it apart and removed

Stephen's leg from its teeth. Every shift appeared to be more harmful than the last as he shrilled in agony.

"Why are you here?" I lost my patience.

"I'd answer that if I were you." Dani backed me up.

"I'm looking for a safe place, that's all. For, for me and my family," he managed to say.

"Well, where's your family?" Lamor asked.

" A day's out. We're not from around her so I stashed them away," Stephen explained

"Where are you from?" I followed up.

"Florida," he responded.

"What part?" I drilled.

"Uh, Jacksonville," he answered.

"Darnell Cookman, Atlantic Coast, First Coast, Sandalwood?" I pressed. He stalled but I didn't. "What's your cause?"

"Amendment 2," he blurted.

"Get up, your leg is fine. Keep it clean and it won't get infected." I put my hand out to help him to his feet. We helped him hop back to camp. We were greeted by Angelique, Sonny and others, guns cocked in our direction. I dropped him in a chair in the middle of the camp. Everyone was quiet and stared on. "Lamor, could you show me where the antiseptic and bandages are?" I lead. Dani played with her knife hovering near the stranger.

Lamor and I created distance between us and the group. "Do you tru—"

"No," I said, knowing where this conversation was going. "We can't trust him. Spittle never shut up about Jacksonville and the high school rivalry games growing up. 'Stephen' didn't recognize any of the schools I named but quickly blurted out his cause as if he practiced it. We can't trust him. But a corpse can't give information, so let's keep an eye out."

Lamor shared my sentiment, "I'll watch him tonight." He said and started gathering supplies to clean Stephen's wounds.

When we returned, part of the crowd dissipated. Angelique held her rifle low and ready anticipating any of Stephen's moves. "So, Stephen. How'd you make it all the way to north Georgia?"

Lamor and I took turns dressing his wounds as Stephen began his story. He explained that since the war he and his family kept trying to make their way north to some relatives in Canada. They hid out in abandoned homes and found food when they could. Lamor propped his foot up on a stump. Stephen shifted in pain, pausing his story.

"So how'd you find our camp?" I bantered.

"The people at the rail yard," he said, certain.

If my organs could fall asleep and get that tingling feeling the way limbs do, like when I sit on my legs or fall asleep on my arms, that's what my insides felt like when he exposed his source. Only, my organs can't fall "asleep." That tingling was *unrest. You slick mother fucker.*

I got up and stomped my way to my cabin. I had to finish this radio. I had to reach Nixon and the group. I could feel Stephen wasn't who he said, but I needed to further prove it. I stayed up all night tweaking components. I tried keying the group over the radio but no response. What felt like a few thousand retests made dark turn to light, and my anger powered it all. I keyed and keyed until finally, I heard some static back. It worked! They heard me and were trying to respond. I needed to fine-tune our frequency, I needed to speak to Nixon, when Lamor burst in. "Freya! He's gone. Stephen is gone and Lynn is missing."

EIGHT

T HAT NIGHT IN THE RAIL yard felt long and cold. None of us slept, although we needed it. It had to be no later than 5:00 a.m. when the shallow grunts of exertion woke me. I waited until my eyes blurred into focus. Sitting up and scanning the trailer, trying to trace the source of noise. Opening the door, I found Spittle drenched in sweat.

"Mornin' sunshine," Spittle said, gleefully. The pattern of his high steps matched rhythmically with his words.

"What's up buddy?" I waited for an explanation.

"I was feeling angsty. When I get the jitters, I work out." His words fell between breathes, without missing a rep of mountain climbers. "Care to join me?" he offered.

Spittle hasn't joined us on missions in the past. So, I knew I had to give him a pass for how ever he chose to rally himself. I sleepily blinked as a response and turned around, closing the door behind me. The moonlight that slipped between the door closing, showed a light on Isaacs face. He too was awake, just lying in stillness. I laid back on the ground, pack propping my head up and stared at the cold steel ceiling.

"She's fine you know," Isaac started.

"What time should we head back?" I asked, dryly.

He got my hint. "I say we eat and get going. Amanda said she could ration us some water for the trip as well."

"Good, good." Was all I could gather to say.

"Let's go, now," another voice added. "I mean sense we're all awake and talking about it anyway." Elise's sarcasm knew no time constraints. I heard her sleep pallet shift as she sat up.

"Okay, then what've we got?" I tasked. We all dug into our bags in that dark room, knowing where our items were. Clinks of cans hit the floor.

"Hey Spit!" Elise yelled out.

Without missing a beat, Spittle entered the trailer. "I'm not used to having woman callers so early in the morn'. I'm not decent." He crossed his hands over his exposed chest.

"Buffet breakfast, dummy." Elise countered.

"Ooo." Spittle was genuinely enthused. "Y'all are gonna like this," he said before revealing an opened package of mini cookies. The group shared an expression of indifference. He grimaced, digging into his bag and pulling out a pouch of cranberries. Which, was met with more acceptance.

We pried open old cans of meat and beans along with dried goods, then began to scarf it down. Over the months, we've been lucky enough to have more common cuisine back at camp, thanks to Kayson. In this moment however, we regretted being so spoiled, our stomachs did too. A few empty cans later I stood up, not being able to stand another bite, and walked outside with my canteen.

The sun was out and slightly cooler than usual. I saw some movement around the camp, and was certain Anthony was one of the early risers. Looking on, I rinsed my mouth out with water, swooshing it around to flush the grime. I pulled an old cloth from my bag, splashing some of the canteen's contents onto it, and began washing my face. The layers of environment and sleep were wiped away. I tried to retain some normalcy, although my body odor reminded me of the alternative. Gravel shuffled under shoes, Elise paralleled herself next to me. I smirked as she began her hygiene regimen, because she was smart enough to bring a toothbrush.

We stood silent with the exception of her brushing. She pulled a small napkin from her pocket, as Isaac walked by grabbing some of its contents.

"Oh, thanks, El," Isaac laughed. She did too. He broke off a small piece of the mint leaf, before offering the remains to me. We each polished it against our teeth. Spittle joined us soon after, patting away the water from his bird bath.

"Let's find Amanda, Anthony and the others." Elise said. "The sooner we can get back to camp the better." We all nodded in agreement. After gathering our gear, we came across Josh first and asked him to point us to Amanda. He, in turn, walked us to her trailer. She had just finished her watch shift and offered us a half smile upon arrival.

"I was expecting you all, but not so soon. Off already?" she asked.

"Yea," Elsie said, shortly.

"We gotta get with our people and prepare." Amanda knew what Elise meant, and shook her head respectfully.

"I got y'all's water right here. I also drew a map of some trails we've used that should get y'all back." Amanda handed Elise a sack.

"Thank you," Elise said warmly.

"Nixon! Guys! Come in, come in!" a shrill voice came through the radio. My adrenaline accelerated. *She did it!*

We all scurried to get the radio. Kneeling down on the ground in both desperation and urgency. Pulling at the bag's zipper, Elise peeled the radio out shouting back, "Hello, hello!" We waited. Nothing.

"Where's your tallest lookout?" Elise demanded to know.

Josh responded, "It's on the backside of camp. It looks over our site and a little beyond the border, but its only about twenty-five feet."

The gears in Elise's mind could be seen turning. Simultaneously we both said, "The train station."

"Is there any access to the train station's roof? It would be in some sort of secured area. A boiler or maintenance room maybe." Her impatience directed at both Amanda and Josh.

"Yes—yes follow me." Josh lead the way. We raced through camp garnishing the attention of Anthony and the others who followed. Running in full stride, we left the perimeter of their camp and darted to the shadows of the train overhang. We stopped at a metal gate wrapped in chains and a lock. Isaac walked forward, slinging his rifle to the front in one motion. He raised it high like a sword and thrusted the stock down into the lock. A loud clank echoed the empty space, followed by chimes of chains being untangled. We opened the gate and all hurried to the stairs we found behind it. One by one we made our way up the access door. Elise turned the hatch until the door gave up its resistance. We climbed onto the old roof and keyed the radio again. Out of breath and trying to swallow to lubricate our words, Elise yelled, "Freya! Freya! Can you hear me?!"

"Damn girl, it's good to hear your voice," Freya responded smoothly. We all released a yell of triumph.

"Freya! We're here. We're all okay. But we're heading back. Somethings not right. Some Scourge refugees are wandering. The message wasn't for us but the warning still applies. We gotta move camp." Elise's words couldn't be said fast enough for her, and stung us all as we listened.

What happened next made our triumph of communication fade fast. Freya said she had a gut feeling when that stranger had showed and she was right. Hearing of Lynn's abduction took ahold of Elise. Isaac took over the radio, to finish detailing the intel we gathered. The rail yard group just stood on in disbelief. We shared that disbelief. Someone came into our home and grabbed one of our own. The same type of someone who didn't deserve our mercies. Anger filled every voided space in me. I looked up searching the sky for a sign, for anything.

Isaac shoved the radio into my chest. "She asked for you," he said taking a few steps back to the group.

"Hey Naz," I said.

"Hey Nix," she patched in, "I think in light of everything. You should leave the boombox and take the radio."

"Right, right," I added in an attempt to be collected. "Are you okay?" I couldn't help myself to inquire.

"I've been better," Freya said admittedly. "You guys just get back here safe. Please."

"We will," I assured. I heard wrestling and turned around to find Josh and Isaac at odds.

"Whoa, what the hell is going on?" I pushed Isaac back.

"We said we wanted to find Lynn and they don't want to back us!" Spittle aggressed.

"Listen we can ration you all with some water and send you on your way but this isn't our fight," Amanda pleaded.

Isaac still lunged forward. "We came all this way to deliver—you know what. We don't need ya." Isaac turned facing me. "That girl back at the outpost said her family was with the Scourge until they wanted them to offer up a sacrifice. If that's true, and the dad took Lynn, then he must be taking her to 7b."

Josh was heated. "Listen. We understand you're upset. But we don't have the numbers or fire power to help, not the way you want us to." Those words stung.

Anthony stood pensively. "We will help you," Anthony said, "But we will not go with you."

Spittle's face began to tense. Patience to hear Anthony out, and an overwhelming disbelief kept us all silent.

"We know where another group is, about sixty miles southwest of us. We will let them know what's occurred. If we can rally our allies, you'll have a better chance of getting the little girl back." Anthony's voice was washed in calmness.

"We don't have time for that," Isaac pushed back. "Lynn could be dead if we wait to have the numbers. This is a search and rescue, not a recovery."

"Listen," Anthony tried again. "We can send some folks to warn and rally others, and I'll go to your camp. I can help organize your people for the journey here."

"The journey here?" My eyebrow raised.

Anthony's arms opened to the camp below us. "We have the space and the borders to keep your people safe. The note urged *us* to move because of the impending attacks. Even though the message was intercepted, its contents are still valid. If you don't go, more of your people will be captured. At least if they come here, we can have the numbers and odds in our favor, for whatever may come."

Isaac and I shared deep eye contact. He was right. We didn't want anyone else to die. We'd been training to fight but didn't want to engage in it. We all have survived so much the last few months. This gave us an out, the out we needed. Elise caught the wrinkles between my brows and knew I was trapped in my thoughts.

She turned to Anthony and said, "You're going to need to bring some people with you. We have a big group." Her head tilted and chin protruded, she took the reins. "The outpost has been compromised but there's a creek there you can travel along," she pointed out. "Break the Refuge up into two caravans. We have some guys back at camp that'll show you the best way. Get our people out first, then some of them can follow up with your guys at the other ally camps." Elise spoke definitively. No one dared a rebuttal. She took a few steps toward Isaac and stared him down as she did. She kneeled and began digging through Isaac's bag. He shifted his stance. "Here," she said, handing Josh the boombox. "Y'all take this, you'll be able to hear us communicate on it. It'll keep you in the loop but you won't be able to talk back." Elise pivoted to position herself near me, but not before sneaking a wink of solidarity. She couldn't have known what Freya said to me. Nonetheless, her instincts of rebellion wouldn't let her hand over the other radio. Feeling supported, I took a step forward.

"Everybody needs to head out in about an hour," I said and continued before Josh could get a word in. "If you guys say you support us, then I need you to do it even when it's not convenient." Anthony and I locked eyes, he stepped forward offering his hand to shake. We embraced briefly.

"We'll go now then, you all stay as long as you need." After Anthony spoke, Josh and Amanda began to follow him off the roof.

"Wait, Amanda!" said Elise. "We're going to need your brain. Tell us everything you remember about the refugees and everything you know about the Scourge."

She complied and said, "Alright, I'll be in my trailer, come find me when y'all are done."

We spent the next thirty minutes on that roof. We called in to Freya, and she was receptive of our plan despite the timeline. She was certain that herself,

Lamor, Kayson, and Dani could get the refuge ready to mobilize before Anthony's arrival. The hesitation only came when she heard that Isaac, Elise, Spittle and I, wouldn't be joining them.

NINE

THIS WAS THE LAST TIME. It had to be. The valor we projected disguised our internal struggle. *Our lives cannot continue like this.* My mind replayed this bad song. Looking at my sister, I hated what this world was doing to her. As twisted irony would have it, coddling her would only disarm her and do a disservice for her survival. She had to be strong. Our adrenaline moved us beyond our hesitations but our eyes couldn't. We agreed to drive directly to the Scourge zone. Spittle and some of the 11D members loaded up some "fun arsenal," as Spittle put it and we all gassed up each vehicle for the ready.

"I know you will get Lynn back." Anthony and my eyes connected as we shook hands. I could only muster a tight lipped grin. Isaac and Elise held a conversation nearby and began waving me over. "Thanks for everything, man." I shook Anthony's hand more firmly.

Approaching Elise and Isaac, they both appeared eager. "We need to get going, bud," Isaac said. I nodded in agreement and looked to Elise.

"You ready?" I pressed.

"Let's go get our girl," Elise said, smoothly.

"You ready?" Isaac pressed me.

"King Kong ain't got shit on me." We let out a roaring laugh. Spittle's confusion surfaced, not understanding the reference. Only making us laugh harder.

"Get your ass in the car," Isaac egged on.

Isaac jumped in the driver's seat and slapped the roof. "Wooo let's go!" He yelled in a battle cry as engines alongside us revved. We all began exiting the steel barriers, out and into our independent directions. Spittle sat shotgun, Elise and I in back. Nervously I began checking my ammo levels. Nothing was going to be left to chance. We knew the trip was maybe only forty minutes by car. In the back of my mind I thought about the Refuge. Anthony and his guys should arrive there closer to thirty minutes. Hopefully, Freya and Lamor had everyone ready.

"Does this thing have any music?" Spittle had to break the silence and began pressing buttons.

Elise ignored him and asked, "So, what's the plan? When we arrive, I mean we can't just knock on the door." She leaned forward hanging on Isaacs seat.

"When I used to do raids, the element of surprise was everything. If we can remain unnoticed. We can get a good idea of where they're holding Lynn. Then bust in there."

"She could literally be anywhere," Spittle said engaged.

"Well, let's follow what we know. We know Charlotte, we know the cars she got grabbed in. If they're holding Charlotte, it's probably in the same place as Lynn." Elise looked over her shoulder at me as I spoke.

"Let's find those SUVs." Elise said. Nods proceeded in unison. We all sunk into our respective thoughts, preparing for what was to come. Spittle radioed Freya as we approached North Fulton county. She said Anthony had arrived and everyone was being loaded up into camp vehicles. I audibly exhaled and Elise shot a smile in my direction. We would be arriving as they were leaving and my focus was now undivided.

Our vehicle slowed the closer we got. Isaac drove more intently and inconspicuously as we passed parked vehicles. The few times we traveled these parts, it astounded me how we grasped at our old shell of society differently. At the refuge we chose humanity and community, we clung to each other. In 7b, they clung to law and order.

I remember the day the economy official shut down. It was all so abrupt. An emergency message broadcast rang a high-pitched tone, alerting everyone to return to their homes and shelter in place. News casters followed up with fear mongered predictions, but I didn't want to take any chances. I spoke to Elise that morning and told her I'd come get her from school. I knew she would be safer with me. Before I could finish packing up the car with gear, my phone rang .

"Uhhh!" A deep tear-filled gasp bled through the speaker.

"Nixon, people are here." Elise belted out. "I hear the yelling downstairs," she said through breathes. Her hyperventilating was deep and washed over in fear.

"STOP! Listen to me. Listen, can you get out?" I demanded.

"No I can't they—" she started to say.

"Do you have the taser I gave you, can you get to the top floor?" I needed to know.

"Yes I—" Elise wailed.

"Go! Go now, go to the top floor and find where your hatch is! It may be a utility closet or laundry room, go now!"

I tried to drive and focus on my phone, the images in the frame changed rapidly as Elise ran for her life.

All I continued to yell was "Elise, I am coming, tell me when you make it there!"

Hearing hurried echoed footsteps in her stair wells incited panic in me as well. *Why was this happening?* I thought, she was supposed to be safe at school.

The images began to steady when she reached the laundry room. A few girls held each other nearby sobbing. She placed the phone flat as I looked up at her and the ceiling.

"Nixon, I found it!" she yelled, her voice became more emboldened. "Wait. It doesn't go to the roof," she said. "It doesn't go out!" Before gloom could creep in I needed her to stay strong.

"Elise go. Go into the attic!" I yelled to the speaker." Turn off the lights in the laundry room. Take off your shoes so they don't leave prints. Everybody throw them in the dryer now!" All the young girls began doing as instructed. Elise hopped off of the machine and began helping girls up one by one. She tugged the bottom of her shirt to wipe the footprint smudges off the dryer top

"Elise, hurry!" She palmed the phone and the screen blurred a pinkish red. I could hear the hatch creak close.

"I'm going to put my phone on mute so you can't hear me, turn your phones off and stay silent." The glare of the screen highlighted her features as she nodded. Emboldened, she wouldn't allow a tear to fall but I could see them resting in her eyes.

I weaved in the street avoiding debris. As I got closer to the city I could hear loud noises coming from the phone. They were muffled and aggressive in tone. I pressed my finger to my lips instructing her to stay quiet. Her tears soon took over her face but she didn't make a sound. Young girls were huddled behind her pressing their palms into their mouths holding in screams. I drove faster.

City streets were filling with masked civilian with bandannas covering half their faces. Some shouted as I drove past. The noise died down on the other end of the phone and I could see Elise physically exhale. The vehicle jerked as I made a sudden stop, parking the car across spaces outside of her building. My hands shook as I texted her "I'm here." Somehow I was able to steady them enough to take my small assault rifle off safety.

I'm thankful every day I made it to Elise in time and before the rebellion got out of hand. When this first unfolded, people were angry and rightfully so. Those who found a target in the rebellion, who thought protesting was unwarranted, who agreed with policing minority groups and other measures of targeted oppression later turned into the Scourge. It was the likes of them who decided to attack Elise's dorm as retaliation. A cowardly directive, instead of facing the protestors in the street. They wanted to attack our sisters and daughters enrolled at the all-girls school.

Over the course of a week, police precincts, big businesses, and monuments of colonial America were set ablaze. One act of revolt after another, the world grew aware of the divide in America. And the focus grew further and further away from what caused it.

Driving into the Scourge limits I couldn't help but remember. Elise's body language was telling, and I could see she remembered too. The trauma and fear she experienced, we experienced, was at the hands of them.

Now driving into city limits, we braced.

We all grew impatient and that intensity filled every seat. All the store fronts turned into townhomes, steps away from a long forgotten bustling city center. Each residence towered between businesses. A yellow, jewel-toned door was dilapidated just enough to show the essence of the previous owner. Yet, the walkway was outfitted with fresh flowerpots, to show the arrogance of the new. Blood-smeared sidewalks and smashed car windows, were mocked by a woman walking her poodle. They lived as though there was no crack in our precious world. This bubble was inflated by ethnocentric ignorance.

Our plights were out of sight, and far from their minds before the revolt. In the aftermath, this remained apparent. Some of the residents were already here and others migrated over. It was infuriating to know, they occupied houses that others were run out of. That they felt safe enough amongst themselves to go out for a walk, while we were hunted into hiding. In an attempt to avoid conflict, we the oppressed, ran to marginal outskirts. While they lived comfortably in developed communities. They lived arrogantly without fear, so why shouldn't we?

Isaac nervously checked the rearview mirror. We partially reached our destination and were uncertain where to go from there. We had to remain close but unseen. "What about there?" Elise pointed over Isaacs shoulder. Ahead of us stood a mid-level hotel. The overhang housed vehicles, clustered together at the abandoned valet podium in front of the hotel entrance. Our truck was just compact enough to tuck behind a contractor van, keeping us camouflaged from the road. We readied ourselves before exiting. We strapped on our backpacks and cemented our weapons to our chests. Prepared to aim and fire as needed. One by one, we went low and maneuvered into the front entrance.

Spittle pried the doors open to find a somewhat clean lobby. He visually cleared the room, before signaling Isaac to join him. Providing cover over each, we made our way to apparent safety. First Spittle, then Isaac, then Elise, and me.

"Maybe we should stay down here, closer to the exits," I encouraged.

"Or maybe we should go to the fifth floor, further from our enemies." Elise countered.

"I'll get better signal up top, the closer to the roof the better." Spittle added.

"Alright, so let's meet in the middle." Isaac mediated. We all took the stairs to the third floor. We took the rooms directly next to the stairs, adjacent to one another. The third floor was high enough to see up the street and clock who was coming and going.

We unloaded our things and needed a brainstorming session. "They have those little soaps and shampoos, dude!" Spittle called from the bathroom. "No! They have running water," he said peeking his head out. "It's been forever since I've taken a shower. I used to do my best thinking in the shower." Spittle said disappointed before joining us on the couch. My jaw tightened hearing of yet another nicety the Scourge enjoys. Isaac only managed to shake his head.

"We can look for the SUVs all day, but we still don't know who was driving. We need to figure out where they are parked so we can see who gets in." I started.

"Oh, well I got that covered. Dani gave me a little hunting gift for our travels." Isaac pulled out a pair of binoculars. A smile broke across my lips, and I quickly covered it to hold in my excitement.

"Good shit, Dani!" Elise chimed in. Grabbing the binoculars from Isaacs hands, Elise went towards the window. She tilted rhythmically going from left to right. Waiting to come across anything noteworthy.

"Well, let me know if you guys find anything. I'm going to take a shower," there was no hesitation as Spittle disappeared into the bathroom closing the door behind him.

"Make it quick!" Isaac yelled, towards the door. " I want to bathe too." He added in a softer tone.

Isaac and I planted ourselves slightly behind Elise, looking out hoping for a clue. Twenty minutes into our stakeout, we each became anxious. Spittle came out to join us, Isaac went on to shower and I took over the binoculars from Elise. I watched until something caught my eye.

"Hey!" I said firmly, "Three cars just peeled the same corner up there. One of them was a wagon." The same wagon we saw at the outpost, cruising, sandwiched between two other vehicles. It had to be Stephen and he must have had Lynn. We dispersed, grabbing all of the ammunitions we could carry. "Bring your weapons and the radios on your person. If it can't fit in pockets, leave it in your bags in the car. We need to be light-footed. Just in case." No one responded but I knew they all understood. Shuffling down the stairs, only the handrails kept my balance. The loud echoes of our steps filled the stairwell. Our adrenaline had to be reeled back, coming to a sudden halt at the exit door. Peeking before exiting, we skimmed around the back of the building. Being sure to walk along the perimeter with no gaps between the building and us, we made our way to the truck. I hobbled to the driving seat, confident with Isaac covering me. I quickly pulled out of the parking lot and drove unsettlingly slowly.

"Nix, what are you doing, they may have Lynn, GO!" Elise heckled from behind.

"We're no good to her if they see us coming, we'll go the way they went and see where they stopped. We can scope it out from there." I assured my sister. Though, I could hear her disagreement in the exaggerated sigh she let out. I made the same turn as the caravan and inched along down the street.

This was certainly a more residential side of the main road. The street narrowed with one lane in each direction. Kids at play signs started to guard the sidewalks and paper windmills trimmed a yard's entrance. Stopping at a four-way intersection, Elise vigorously tapped my shoulder, pointing down the left side of a cul-de-sac. Those were the vehicles. *The cars were parked right there*, my mind digested. The lump in my throat couldn't be swallowed and my palms began to sweat.

I continued traveling forward. Never breaking my glance, I said, "We'll park a few streets up and go in from the backside. We need as many odds in our favor as possible." Continuing on, we splashed our way through runoff puddles before making a right down a forgotten cul-de-sac.

We found a small cottage and pulled into its driveway. The homes on this street never experienced gentrification, dated pre-war and it showed. Isaac hopped out to manually lift the garage door so we could park inside. Turning off the engine, I folded my hand over the door handle and leveraged my weight against it. Each of us exited. Spittle pointed towards the door leading into the home. Sandwiched between the vehicle and cold cement walls, we sidestepped to the door, handguns unholstered.

With a swift kick, the door was opened and we bled into the space, room to room. "All clear," we each echoed. Every room was flipped and awry. Sofas, mattresses, and dressers all disoriented in their respective spaces. We couldn't dwell on what evidently occurred, only what was next to come. Looking through the kitchen window we could see a short wire fence lining the perimeter. The home directly behind us appeared vacant, but the only way of knowing was to enter. Elise looked to me and nodded, she was ready so I had to be.

"We'll go first," I said to the others. Elise lunged through the exit, barrel leading the way. I pushed passed the door frame to follow and clenched the back of her shirt. Facing the rear, being sure not to lose her, I scanned to cover our backs looking to the sides of the house Isaac and Spittle couldn't see. El's route was precise and calculated. She was so smart and more than well adapted at this point. Without sharing a glance, we stopped and I knew we were at the fence. I took a knee and took aim at the uncharted house. Elise hopped the fence and crouched down with finesse. Shooting an inquiring stare at Isaac, I leaped over after receiving a two finger point of approval. We pressed to the back of the home, quickly scanned the windows and saw it appeared vacant too. I bent my arm high enough for Isaac to see and waved it in a circular motion, we were ready to rally. Isaac and Spittle started towards us, as Elise and I provided cover. Once our team was reunited, it gave us the confidence to continue.

We split along the sides of the house, ducking well below each window as we passed. Spittle and Isaac on one side, Elise and I on the other, we were too far away to speak yet visible enough to communicate. Remerged and ready at the front of the house, apprehension built a wall in front of me. A man stood across the avenue, in his front yard. Back facing us, he watered his plants oblivious to our presence. Crouched behind garbage bins, I looked across the matchbox home to Isaac, lying flat behind overgrown shrubs.

Spittle hovered nearby, tapping Isaac to get his attention. "Move?" he questioningly mouthed. I continued to scan the street. I looked at Isaac who signaled a retreat back and I nodded. Before I could fully adjust from kneeling Elise forcefully grabbed my shoulder. I looked at her before following her pointed finger.

She whispered in my ear, "Look." I continued to look along the wide width home before she finished, "Those plants don't need any more water." I noticed water pooled at the base of the driveway and down the street.

"That's a post." I said looking back at her.

She nodded yes. We retraced to the rear of the home.

Spittle looked at us impatiently, "What's up?"

"That guy is bullshit," Elise inserted. "Did you see how drenched the yard was, there's no way he's just watering plants. Had to of been standing there for a while, he's a look out."

Spittle looked to Isaac. "Let me get those sights up off you buddy." Isaac pulled the binoculars out of his cargo pocket. Spittle shuffled to the edge of the house and laid flat. He looked on as we covered the area around us. After a short time, Spittle got up shuffling back over to us.

"There's two guys in the front room, and who knows how many more throughout the house. Safest bet? We can get past them if we take a wide route to the house where the cars are parked."

"But we'll have a better vantage point if we can go to the SUV house *directly* from behind," Elise countered.

"Exactly," Spittle began, "If you ask me, I say we flank 'em. Go wide in a rectangle pattern to take the landscaper out from the sides, and go to the big house from their own backyard. They wouldn't expect the lookout house to get overrun, let alone be the point of entry to take them out."

As much as I hated to say it, my lips uttered, "Spittle's right. Let's do it." I tapped my chest and pointed to Spittle. Without saying more, we were on him, and I trusted we could take his lead. Spittle swiped his nose and fell into his role. Pointing one way east and then west, again we split into pairs. We each moved laterally into neighboring yards. Every gap was a possibility of exposure, no one took it lightly. One by one we tiptoed across landscapes and fences to create a greater space between where we started. We reached a position of maybe four yards apart. Spittle stood tall and signaled us to move forward, he pressed, and we did the same. We crept through the side yard, onto the front lawn. With the street directly in front of us, we hoped we were far enough out of the unseen guards peripherals. I saw Isaacs frame move from the house's shadows to a tree mid-lawn, and on to a streetcar. Spittle inched the same path and I knew Elise and I had to move once he was safe.

We had no time for anything other than quick evaluation. The cluster of potted plants near the driveway had to do. I sprinted across to the yard's property line to take cover. Without vehicles nearby, the picket fence across the street was the only other option. I peeked out to see Spittle crossing the street into the adjacent yard, then back to see Elise joining me. It all happens so quickly, but overthinking would insight fear. So, I just went. At full sprint, I lunged into the grass and made it behind the picket fence. I aimed my rifle at the lookout through the gapped wood planks, prepared to cover Elise. She took the cue and ran to me, slamming into my side unable to stop her momentum.

"What do you see?" El asked in shaken breaths.

"Spit and Isaac are closing the gap towards the house, we gotta move." The curvature of the home gave us the cover we needed. Synchronized steps and stealth coordination propelled us on. We glided past porches and windows until we stood on the neighboring property, stalled one yard away. There was no going back, nor did any of us intend too. The closer we came the tighter I held my pistol grip. The large-build lookout continued on watering the shrubs and scanned around him every so often. He looked in our direction, then over to the guys. I grabbed Elise and started to move. Running into the side scape driveway, we barely remained out of sight. We glued our bodies against the brick house, knowing the unidentified man was nearest to us. We made it.

Although, the celebration was short-lived as I heard the garden hose spout hit the pavement. Peering around the corner, the man was charging in Isaac and Spit's direction. "Fuck." I whispered. Before he could make his way down the long walkway, muscle memory sent me after him. I couldn't let him make it to the front windows of the house. I had to stop him. My steps got heavier and he heard me coming. Turning around he threw a heavy punch in my direction. I grabbed his hand after the failed punch and cupped it over my pistol barrel. I leaned into the advantage, raising the back of his hand to his forehead, and gingerly squeezed the trigger. The shot was muffled by his cotton gloves and the fat of his flesh. As his legs gave out beneath him, I felt Elise helping me catch his fall, and saw Isaac running across the grass. He made it to the front door ahead of us and entered in a blaze. The crashes of furniture and booms of bodies could not be mistaken. Elise entered first, as I covered her, then I followed shortly after. Blood smeared across the carpet, Isaac had a guard facedown near his slain associate.

"Where's the girl?" demanded Isaac.

The guard laughed. "She doesn't want to be saved. She's saving us. Righting *your* wrongs"

"Kill 'em," Spittle said abruptly. "Kill this guy, before I—" he started to pace.

Isaac began to pull the trigger, until Elise kneeled down by his head. "Are they keeping her over there?" she pointed through the yard with her knife. He only looked down. "They are, aren't they? Well good. Once we get her, I'll let them know you made the ultimate sacrifice." Her blade entered his neck and recoiled from the blood thrush. He gargled on his blood, trying to find air.

"Come on, El," Isaac pleaded. She shot him a grimace before diving her blade through the guard's inner ear, killing him instantly. I stared on watching her anger manifest.

"Marry me, mama," Spittle snickered to himself.

"Let's go!" Elise directed. The house was wider than it was deep. A few steps and we stood near the back door. The back of the house was wrapped by a long sunroom, just beyond the kitchen. Spittle pulled the binoculars out and proceeded with surveillance.

"I see nothing," he said, dismissively.

"What do you mean, nothing?" I asked of him.

"I see nothing. No movement, no guards, no trucks."

"Great," Isaac said, sarcastically.

"Let's go!" Elise said again.

"Go *what,* El?" I pushed.

"Go *look!* Go track Lynn! Kill the Scourge. Go do something. Because changing the plan *now* will leave us with less of a lead than we have. We can look through the house and maybe find answers." Elise's passion was not lost on anyone. Her words were broken in their delivery. Only echoing her current state of emotion. It could had been Elise a few months ago, she better than most understands the fear Lynn probably feels not knowing what harm may come.

I slapped her arm in assurance, hoping to also jolt her back into composure. We readjusted ourselves and weapons before exiting the back door. It was a straight dash to the large home behind us. Each of us ran in full sprint. The backyards were separated by sparse trees and a shallow irrigation creek. None of which posed too great of an obstacle. Heading straight towards the basement door, the double deck above shielded us from all view.

"I'll go around front," Elise announced before rounding the hill.

"I got her," Spittle said before following her up. Backing away and a swift kick to the frame. Isaac entered the basement. A toppled chair and chains greeted us in a bare cement room. The insulation was incomplete and the stair frame led up to an open door. The footsteps above us let me know they made it inside okay. "Clear!" We each began yelling out moving to each of the three levels. The basement had a room with a mattress on the floor and bolt locks on the door. I returned to it, once we confirmed the house was vacant. It smelled of urine and the source was traced to a puddle in the corner. I stood there staring in disbelief until Spittle yelled from above.

"Hey y'all, come here." We each reemerged finding him in the kitchen. Drawer pulled open, we were all unsure what to make of it.

"What the hell?" Isaac said, confused. Locks with keys, codes, and zip ties were stuffed inside. Different shaped locks and sizes all stocked and on standby.

"There's a room downstairs. Looks like they were holding someone but the door had bolt locks."

"Why have all these locks if they're not using them? They have to be using them." Elise pieced together.

"They're definitely using them," I said without a doubt.

"Wherever they are using them, it's not here. But why would they need so many?" Isaac added.

"Ya think they have more captives?" Spittle asked.

"If so, wouldn't there be more rooms here like the basement, or more houses like this?" Isaac inquired of the group.

"No. Because it would spread out too much of their manpower. More houses means more posts. Then, having multiple uncivil captives in one house would be a risk to uprising. None of which would be good for the Scourge and none of it still explains the locks." Elise's face remained puzzled.

"What if they're not in a house, but they are *being* housed?" I led on.

"Being housed?" Elise followed up.

I nodded, "Yeah. I think I know where Lynn is."

TEN

MAKING OUR WAY BACK, I was dazed. Weaving between streets back to where we started, no one spoke. Isaac took control upon arrival and jumped into the driver's seat.

"Let's go to the commercial side and industrial side," Elise said joining me in the backseat. "If there are any storage facilities here, that's probably where they're at." Elise spoke passionately, her stare never wavering from my direction. I was partially sure we would find her in a storage locker. I had hoped I was right and hoped I was wrong all in the same sequence. I just wanted to get out of here, get Lynn out of here. We creeped along, encountering more passersby along the way. Two vehicles caught my attention when we yielded at an intersection. Parked along the side of the road was a vehicle all too familiar, being approached by the passengers of another.

"The cavalry's here!" Spittle announced, more enthused than I.

"That's—it's Freya," I scoffed, I couldn't believe what I was seeing. The SUV had four shadows inside. I could only assume Dani, Lamor, and Kayson joined her for the ride. What were they thinking? The Scourge patrol car had them pulled over. Complying made them appear less threatening, but was possibly a death sentence. We stayed as long as we could at the stop. Long enough to see the Scourge members at Freya's and the passenger window. Long enough to see Dani and Lamor exit the vehicle and load into the Scourge's. With the incident in our rearview, my gut turned over in angst. The car was quiet.

"Where's the radio?" I inquired of Isaac.

"Do you think that's a good id—" Isaac began.

"Give me the goddamn radio, Isaac," I sliced back. Isaac rustled in his bag to turn it on before handing the radio back to me.

"Freya, Freya!" I repeated into the mic. I let go of the call key and waited.

"Where have you been?" Freya transmitted back. "I tried radioing you guys. Dani and Lamor are in trouble, *they* want to *talk* to them, asked us to follow. Where are you?" Her words were rushed and somewhat rattled.

"The radio was off, it wasn't safe. We just saw everything. What are you doing here? Where are they taking them?" My mind couldn't catch up to the current circumstances.

"We came to help. We couldn't let y'all do this alone. But now, I... I don't know. They said they wanted to register them because they didn't recognize us. I told them we would follow, but they insisted one of us ride with them. Dani wouldn't let Lamor go alone so they both went." Her worry further presented itself.

"You did the right thing. Killing them out in the open would have drawn too much attention. Just follow closely and try not to raise any alarms." I said, attempting to calm her.

"Where are you guys?" Freya questioned again.

"We think Lynn is being kept in a storage yard. Her and maybe more. We'll call if we run into any issues," I said shortly.

"Okay." Freya confirmed. "We'll do the same."

Ending the conversation felt too final. I said nothing more and refocused on our journey. Elise shifted in her seat, avoiding what she overhead. Isaac continued on, towards the warehouse district. It was oddly still and deserted. The streets were covered with natural debris resembling an old dirt trail long forgotten. As we approached the warehouses we saw their gates were overgrown with weeds. Tree branches and gravel crunched beneath our tires, adding traction to pavement. Open bay doors could be seen from the parking lot, it appeared to be pillaged through and a dead end on our rescue mission.

"Should we check it out?" Spittle asked of the group.

"I'll have a quick look just to see," Elise volunteered.

"No, I'll go," I trumped.

"No!" Elise said, pushing my chest into my seat. "*I've* got it"

"No worries Nixon, I'll go with her," Spittle assured before exiting.

I leaned into the window watching Elise and the surrounding environment.

Isaac and I scanned, crossing sites. "You're not doing her any favors." Isaac baited.

"Who?" I asserted.

"Your sister, Naz, you pick. You're not doing either one any good being overprotective and trying to be a halfcocked hero."

"What are you—" I blurted out.

"Brotha' don't bullshit me. I know, El is your sister. You love her and want to protect her. You love

Naz, and for whatever reason neither of you will address that, fine. I get you not wanting anything to happen to them, but acting on emotion will get you killed. Trying to intervene and protect them at every turn is stupid, and will get you killed. For some reason you half enjoy throwing yourself in the fire, when no one asks you to. El, Naz, they're way smarter than either of us. Shit, at this point, I'm more confident in *them* protecting us."

We shared a brief laugh, though I still wasn't privy to his point. Isaac continued, "They're tougher than you give them credit for being. When Angelique and I got married, ya know what she told me?" He paused before breezing past his rhetorical question. "She said 'Love me enough to leave me be. 'I had to learn when to step back and give her the space to do her thing. I'm just saying, love them, and protect them without minimizing their strengths. They know when they got it, and if they don't, they'll say so."

My head tilted back, embracing the chill of leather against my neck. I never considered myself a martyr. Was my silent resentment towards our new world, or feeling like I had to be omnipresent in it? Elise has never required anything of me, yet I've built a narrative of her well-being being my responsibility. *But wasn't it?* She's my baby sister. Did I resent the act or feeling like I had to act?

I studied Elise when she returned to the back seat. I gave my best effort to hear beyond the noise in my head. "No trace of hostages, just remnants of looters," she informed us casually. Spittle inaudibly concurred.

Isaac understood the cue and shifted gears, literally and figuratively. He turned the wheel counterclockwise, looping us around in a tight radius. We wheeled on through the entrance gate, onward down the road.

"I'll hit the boulevard, we can see what we run into from there." Isaac said. I sat battling my nature, in what to do once we arrived. Looking to Elise, she cradled her rifle in her lap, consumed in what was to come.

"It's a storage facility. We just pulled in nearby. It's on J. Carter next to an old school and farmers market, get here." A voice blistered through the radio.

The pace of Freya's voice insisted urgency. We each shot stares throughout the vehicle, and knew better than to respond back. The pressure of Isaac's foot on the accelerator could be felt through the engine's revolution. Enough ground couldn't be covered, no matter how much we willed it to be. Speeding through backroad industrial streets, we neared twice as fast. Reality must have grabbed hold of Isaac, because he slowed before we reached the boulevard. Finally making the turn, we scanned each side of the street. It was unsettling to see the number of Scourge members out civically. Reality got ahold of me too as my chest tightened. *Self-Storage* the sign read. Spittle gestured to veer right. I could see Isaac's hesitation as he shifted the wheel. There were more cars than I cared to count. All here, where we needed to be the most unseen.

Elise had no qualms about the presence of others. "Hide in plain sight boys," she said. She threw her rifle to the floor and concealed her handgun in her waistband. Tucking her knife in her sock, she tapped the back of Spittle's headrest. "Spit, let me get those shampoo bottles you took from the hotel."

"What shampoos?" he started to say, before pulling one out and handing it over. Elise began dabbing the contents throughout her thick hair and neck.

"Here!" she insisted to me. "We'll be less noticeable if we smell and look somewhat clean. Spittle's showering may actually come in handy," She mocked instinctively.

Isaac smirked, "I'm good then."

I shrugged and began lathering chain hotel shampoo on my hands and face. Watching patrons pass us by, Elise looked determined. "Spittle and I will go in first and you two follow shortly after. We split up but maintain visibility. There's gotta be a reason all these people are here and I doubt it's anything good."

We never did hold back hard truths. Hearing what Isaac had to say a short while ago forced me into silence. Not objecting to Elise, when every atom in me yelled that I should, was debilitating. Seeing my restraint, Elise embraced her ascendency. Spittle continued concealing his weapons in preparation for their exit. Elise tapped his shoulder and they both opened their doors without saying a word. The tinted glass separated us, I could see El but she didn't see me. Elise stared at her reflection in the window, confidently and assured. She was seeing *herself,* all her jadedness and rough edges turned into a weapon. Prepared to use it as a self-appointed liberator.

She pulled her hair up into a ponytail and her shirt down over her belt. Riffling through the crowd they both began to blend in. Isaac looked at me in the rear view mirror, and questioned in a sigh, "You ready, buddy?"

ELEVEN

I T WAS A SPAN OF abandoned supercenters and businesses, one after the next. Under the circumstances, being here made me more on edge. Isaac and Nixon weren't answering our transmissions and we were deep in the city of our enemies. Sonny sat next to me in the passenger seat. Dani leaned forward between us, rambling on but her words were lost on me. I couldn't help but fixate on all of our misfortunes. Our group again displaced, running out of fear and terror. This felt familiar, like the beginning, before the revolt broke out; that's not okay. And Lynn, poor Lynn didn't deserve this. The heartbreak of her mother is a cry I hope to never hear again. She trusted us to bring her back. We said we would bring her back. Anything less is not an option.

"Naz, you good?" Lamor pressed.

"Yeah, yeah I'm good." I said looking over to Sonny. My smile tried to convince him and myself. He politely smiled back, offering a gesture of support.

"How do you think everybody's doin? You trust that Anthony guy?" Dani spewed out casually.

I noticeably paused. "Elise seems to," I said. "And I'm good with that. Plus, if they get out of line, Angelique and Dr. Van can handle it."

"The sooner we get in, the sooner we all can get out and get back," Sonny said.

" Did Spittle say where they were going?" Lamor continued.

"Nope," I responded. "Just that they were almost there, I told him we would follow up once we got everyone at camp squared away."

"Well, that was almost an hour ago, and they haven't answered since." Dani recounted the obvious.

"Try again." I requested. Dani leaned further forward to get the radio off the dash.

"Nothin'," she announced after a few moments of keying, then handing it to Sonny.

My mouth grew dry with no response, as an SUV began tailing behind me. I stiffened and everyone took notice. "Put your seatbelts on." I said. My eyes squinted into the rearview. Dani turned her head to see what I was seeing, then turned around with an equally piercing stare.

"Everybody be cool," Lamor instructed. Then the SUV began to flash at me. Off and on, their brightest lights glared into my mirrors. Sonny shuffled to put the radio in the glovebox. "Be cool," Lamor repeated for good measure.

I began to break to choose a safe place to park. With our vehicle slowed to a stop, I shifted to park, and my adrenaline made my knee shake. They stopped behind me and two of them exited. I rolled my window down, leaving the engine running as a precaution. His shadow approached the window before he did, and I could hear cold metal clink from Dani taking precautions of her own. He squared himself to the window, his palm pressed over top of the door. When he leaned in, I prepared myself for our threatening exchange to occur in my personal space.

"Good morning ladies and gents." His words were equally as curious as his eyes. "Can we help you with anything?" On cue, another figure appeared opposite Sonny's window, he ignored him.

"Um, no. Thank you." I said tightly, forcing a smile. "We're just passing through. Making our way south."

"South ya say? Well good, good." He looked up over the vehicle, to his associate.

"You all mind if we register ya? Just a little paper trail we're building for when the world wide web is back up." He tried to sound non-threatening. "It's just for us to know *who* is who, when our lives get back to, you know."

His nonchalant banter on the war of months passed infuriated me. All I could manage to say was, "Oh?"

"Yeah, we'd just need to take you over to the old grade school." He began eyeing the backseat.

"Alright, we'll follow you." I said bluntly.

"Ah naw, I'm afraid you'll have to ride with. Otherwise, he may not believe ya to be friendly." He said gesturing to the other Scourgeman. "It's a part of our verification."

"How about you fella," he continued, pointing to Lamor.

"How about me, what?" Lamor countered.

"You friendly?" the man asked. "How about you come with us, I insist."

"I think he's good, bad back and all." Dani interjected.

"That's alright, we've got comfy seats and padded headrests." The man was relentless.

The eerie silence that proceeded only thickened the tension.

"Alright," Lamor said between clenched teeth. He hid his anger, as we all were enraged.

"I'll go!" Dani said abruptly. I looked at her in the rearview. "I'd like to see these comfy seats, especially after this road trip." A fake laugh ended the sentence.

The man seemed amused, but not as amused as Dani was with herself.

"How about you *both* come," he mandated, stepping back from the vehicle.

Dani looked to Lamor giving his hand a reassuring squeeze before hopping down, out the truck. Lamor got out on his side and slammed the door behind him. My heart raced in a maddened state. Sonny was silent, watching Lamor walk away and grow smaller in the side-view mirror. I needed to think, but my short progress was interrupted by a slight horn honk. The SUV veered left, pulling in front of me. I shifted out of park, then followed closely behind.

I heard my name faintly being called out. Glancing over at Sonny, he wasn't the source but his eyes were big. "Nixon!" I said as Sonny reached into the glove compartment. He keyed the radio for me and held it within talking distance. "Where have you been?" I burst angrily, although I was happy to hear his voice. As the conversation went on, my concerns for their safety were eased. *At least they found us.* I tried to reconcile in my mind. Yet, my concern for Dani and Lamor's safety was only building. Ending the radio call, I tried to re-engage. My thoughts remained fast, so I chose to remain silent.

"It's going to be fine," Sonny attempted to comfort. "We're all in contact and Dani and Lamor can handle themselves. Let's focus on finding Lynn."

Silence was all I could offer in response.

He was right and he knew it, but Sonny's words had no time to stick. After a few short minutes, we arrived.

Alongside a busy intersection, stood a sign that read SEAWIND SCHOOL NEXT RIGHT. What was more interesting was the sign's location. A few yards opposite the parking lot it stood, in front of a shipping store and storage yard.

"Freya, is that it?" Sonny said eagerly, "That has to be it."

"I think so," I said almost grinning. "What are these people doing here?" My expression quickly faded. Sonny and I stared along, as long as we could before turning.

The SUV entrapping Lamor and Dani continued to follow the wind of the road. Landing us suddenly in an old bus loop of a small school. Their brake lights glowed, when a hand waved us forward. Sonny rolled his window down to hear, "Park in there." Being yelled by the driver. Taking the second half of the loop in leisure, I asked Sonny to key the radio one more time. I tried to release my thoughts before I parked, and before the unnamed men grew impatient. I urged Nixon to get here quickly. We had no time for a general radio exchange, so after I spoke I needed no reply. Sonny took my cue and turned the radio off. "That storage facility has to be it, especially with its proximity to their hub. I just hope they get here soon." I said to Sonny, still needing no reply.

As I parked, he hid the radio in the floorboards. We walked towards the school and moved with urgency to get to our friends.

Lamor was always a man of few words but his expression said enough.

"Follow us," the driver said, walking towards what appeared to be a front office.

We entered more pessimistic than ever. A fair-haired woman greeted us with a cheery drawl. "Hey there Troy, Henry, who do you have here?"

"Just some travelers. They were coming from the perimeter so we stopped 'em. Turns out they're some of us." He scanned Lamor from heel to crown. "Wanted to document other allies in the area."

"Oh, well I see. Go ahead and start then," she opened her arm towards a conference room. "I'll keep these two company."

The men nodded and led Lamor and Dani down a hallway.

"Are ya thirsty? We've got water, sweet tea…" she asked of us. Sony and I both passed on the offer and welcomed the lack of conversation that followed.

"So. Where are ya from originally?" She tried to make small talk.

"Virginia, but I've been in Georgia some years now," Sonny stated.

"And you missy? I'm sure you're not from here." She directed her observation to me.

"I was born forty minutes west of here," I said without looking at her.

"Right. Right! But where are you *from*?" She emphasized her words, expecting a different answer.

"Where are you from?" I asked of the stranger.

"Oh right here honey, I'm a pure blood American." The woman stated proudly.

"Well I'm sure she's proud to have you," I said boldly.

"Pardon?" Her senses caught on

More time had gone by than what was comfortable, and Dani and Lamor still hadn't returned. "Where are our friends," I pushed.

"Oh they're probably held up in processing," she said, too instantly. Her mouth maintained a smile but her eyes were shotty. I followed her gaze to a hallway leading back into an unseen space.

"How much longer do you think they'll be?" I questioned.

"Oh, not much longer." The woman said in jest.

I was growing impatient. Sonny just sat, never breaking his stare in her direction.

She apparently grew impatient, standing up to announce, " I'm going to get a snack, I'll be right back."

After she was out of sight, I conversed with Sonny, "I think we should go."

"I'm ready." Sonny said without any further discussion. We got up and walked out, when a shrill voice yelled after us.

"Where ya going?"

"We've gotta go," I asserted.

"Aw sweetie, I can't let you do that." I turned to face her. She flashed me a gun from her bag.

Walking towards her, I displayed defeat. Sonny stood frozen in the hall. She opened her arm back towards the room and I half entered. Standing a foot away, I shifted my weight. Planting my foot behind hers, I pushed her to counter her balance. I maneuvered my way behind her frail frame and locked my forearm around her neck. She clawed my arm and reached for the gun, deciding between air and a weapon to save her life. Sonny took the gun out of her reach and I restrained tighter, blocking her air flow. The strikes grew weaker as her body turned limp, and I let her drop to the ground.

"Bring the truck around," I gave Sonny the keys. "Grab the rope too, we can tie her up, find Lamor and Dani and go." He nodded and walked to the door.

I jetted behind her desk opening drawers and cabinets, pillaging through everything to avoid any surprises. I found more guns, ammo, and cuffs. Filling my cargo pants, I took what I could carry. When Sonny returned, he pulled the truck directly in front of the entrance and entered with fury. Sonny picked up her unconscious body and brought her to a hallway bathroom. He tied her feet and I cuffed her hands behind her back around a grab bar. "Let's do it." I said. Plowing down the hallway we opened door after door with our guns drawn.

The final door was a backroom, common area. It was seemingly empty until we heard a low groan. Just beyond a round table, Dani laid clinging to the floor. Her face was bloodied and shirt torn. She looked up to me with blood-washed eyes, "They took him." Pointing to a side door. Sonny handed her his green bandana to wipe her eyes and they both began dabbing cloth over her gashes.

I peered out the side door window, hoping we had no more threats. The door offered access to the rest of the school; a hall laced with classrooms.

My cheek yielded to the cold steel door. I pressed my face against the pane hoping to get a better vantage point. No one was there. Or so I thought. A set of eyes fixated on me in the corner of a window. Small and sensitive but brilliant enough to take notice. "Dani, are you going to be good?" I asked continuing to look out the window.

"Yeah, I'm good," she confirmed.

"Good, because I think we have company," I replied.

Sonny and Dani didn't hesitate to join me at the exit. I held my gun up against my shoulder and pushed the door open, extending my firing position. There was still no one in the hall. Rushing to the door's window I scanned the inside and gasped. "It's children!" I looked back to my group and they stared in disbelief.

"What?" Dani said.

I jiggled the door handle and to my surprise it was unlocked. When I opened the door, shrieks and screams greeted us. "It's okay, it's okay we're not here to hurt you," Sonny said, putting away his gun. Dani and I followed his lead. The average age in the room couldn't have been older than six. There were many and all were afraid.

I approached one young boy and tried to become acquainted, "My name is Freya, these are my friends." I waved to Sonny and Dani. "What's your name?"

"Cole," he said.

"Well, Cole. I promise I am not here to hurt you, I just want to know what you're doing here." I tried my best to sound nurturing.

"We were chosen—" he started to say.

"Where did you get this?" Dani asked forcefully, holding a purple headband. Her abrasive tone startled the room. The inquiry was directed at a small girl nearby.

"Dani, you're going to scare her," I said pulling her arm back.

"I'm not trying to scare you. I'm just trying to find my friend. Where did you get this?" Dani tried again.

"A girl. She gave it to me. She told me to stop crying," the young girl said.

"Where is she?" Dani asked.

"She left. To save them," the young one confirmed.

"Save them? Save who?" I asked urgently. Her demeanor began to hermit. So, I pried softly, "Where is she saving them?"

Her eyes watered with each blink, she pointed "Next door, at the offering."

Dani made an attempt to outrun me in a sprint towards the door. Neither of us could escape that room fast enough. Sonny offered the children reassurances before we peeled him away. His guilt spoke more than his rationale and he soon paid for it. These poor kids, their eyes remained glued to us, hoping for instruction. However, we had none to offer. All that could be said before we left was, "We're sorry. We're so sorry."

Barreling down the hall, all I could think was… *would we make it?*

TWELVE

T HE CROWD AND MY IMPATIENCE grew sparse. I could still make out the shape of Elise's head in the crowd, yet she was too far for my comfort. Isaac, sensing my discomfort as we watched them turn a corner, began opening his door to get out. Grateful for his initiation, I got out too.

We funneled through the gates as everyone else did, but progressing slowly and observing everything. Curious, I asked, "Where did everyone go?" Isaac pointed ahead and bent his wrist to the left. Inching closer, the smell of baked bread filled our noses. I felt I wasn't moving fast enough until I couldn't move at all and stood frozen in place. Standing in the intersection, I couldn't help but be stunned by the spectacle. Vendors. People selling fresh pretzels, popcorn and pressed juice. Others, perusing through, window-shopping, deciding if their object of barter is congruent.

"You still think she's here?" Isaac inquired in a low tone.

"Now, I'm not sure," I said.

The channel became less congested the further we walked. The end of the aisle exposed a wide open square lot with rows of storage units in three directions. People lined the perimeter of the space and I could see Spittle across the way.

I began to overhear the conversation of the woman behind us, gushing over today's "service." My eavesdropping returned no clarity for the situation we found ourselves in. "Let's make our way over to El and Spit just in case." I suggested to Isaac. Approaching their space, our intention was interrupted.

"Excuse me everyone, excuse me. Thank you all so much for coming. As you know my name is David and I thank you for joining us for today's service. Before we begin, I ask that you all join me in prayer."

My distrust for all in attendance wouldn't allow me to close my eyes. Peaking at the group, they shared my cautions.

"Dear Father, thank you for delivering our enemies. Thank you for not forsaking us. Allow us to continue your works and bring glory back to our world, ah-men," David said in a thunderous voice.

Clinks and thuds repeated in echoes, and figures floated behind the layers of the crowd. Unit by unit the figures walked unhinging each door, dropping the locks to the ground. They then disappeared into the rows of storage behind the main event space to finish their work. David continued talking, but I was too focused on what was behind each door. Trying to move slowly, not to draw unwanted attention, Isaac and I retreated to the outskirts of the audience. "Excuse me," was offered in hushed tones more often than I cared for. These people didn't deserve my respect or courtesies. I wished we could rid the world of them all, but that had to wait for another occasion.

David was long-winded, but that gave us the time to maneuver our way to Elise.

"Service is always a special day to me, because it is rooted in selflessness. As we have all learned in these tragic times, a large portion of our society is selfish and entitled!" His words daggered into the crowd. "Because of the old ways, we are here now, doing as our god ordained. We must not only smite those who hold disdain for the greater good, we must rise against all who oppose making our world clean." David's voice cracked with anger and obscurity.

"We understand from our new interpretation that god has delivered our enemies into our hands. But it doesn't stop there my friends, we have to do our part.

We now know that spirit isn't just what's inside of us, it's an acronym for our mission. Sequence, Plane, Interval, Realm, Interstitial, Time. In order to be with god and have his grace return, we must align ourselves with the mission. We must have full dominion over ourselves and our choices down to the atom. This is the only way to step into our inner power. To remain dominant. We must not succumb to emotions like fear or selfishness, or instinct. What better way to prove our commitment to the mission than true sacrifice. A sacrifice of ourselves." His wingspan opened wide as onlookers began to clap. Elise's eyes were fixed on me as we went to the next aisle and she and Spittle followed. We could hear David continue his speech in the background, but we knew we didn't have much time.

"Let start looking, we gotta get her now," Isaac said.

Elise and Spittle went on to an unoccupied row. The shadow group had already once-overed each unit and left them unlocked. Slowly, Spittle lifted a door and behind it was a woman. On her hands and knees, crouched fully over and drenched in sweat, the cage she was housed in didn't afford much mobility. The unit reeked of urine and feces. She must have been there for days. Elise squeezed her nose between her thumb and index finger, trying to cut off the scent. The woman never flinched. Her dazed confusion kept her from any hope of escape. Spittle slowly rolled down the sheet metal door, becoming numb.

"We've got to find Lynn," Elise urges.

"Lynn, honey. Lynn, respond if you hear us. Lynn," airily we all yelled. Trying to appear like casual patrons we strolled the aisle. Still whispering Lynn's name to no end. Spittle gave soft knocks on the door enough to rattle a response out of its occupants.

"Lynn!" I pleaded, but nothing. Then, between the silence of our calls, I heard a muffled yell. "Did ya hear that?" I asked Isaac, he just nodded as he scanned the row. Isaac continued moving, trying to locate the sound's source.

"Hey!" A small man called out, startling us all to turn in his direction. He slowly began limping over. "What's your business?" He presses out of suspicion.

"Just checking things out for the service," Spittle said without missing a beat.

"Well the list is already posted and it'll go in order, nothing to see." He flapped his arms, directing us back to the main square. Our collective hesitation only seemed to make the small man more irate, "Now." he added impatiently.

Spittle began to deflect, "What happened to your leg there, buddy?" Approaching his personal space, he couldn't look at Spittle with his answer.

"Never mind that," he said. Spittle and Isaac inched past him unnecessarily, and began to walk first. A few steps behind, Elise and I walked out of the row, tailing them and the stranger. Now four rows off the main event, we took our time on the way back.

"Nix," I can hear a faint yell. Panicked, I spun to find her. "Nix," Freya called to me again. She, Dani and Sonny were briskly making their way to us.

I was halfway to her before realizing there was more to her sentence. "Nix, that's him. That's Stephen." I felt cold immediately. The sight of Freya must have spooked him as he tried to scurry on ahead of us. From where I stood, Spittle couldn't have taken more than two giant steps before he reached Stephen. His thick bicep wrapping around his neck and dragging him into another row out of sight from the aisle. All of us ran to where they stowed away. Color flushed Stephen's face from pink to dark maroon. Throwing the weight of his small frame, scratching at Spit's arm to let go, he did all he could to pry free. His leverage was nonexistent and proved no match to Spittle's strength. Freya, then Dani and Sonny, came rushing around the corner just when Spittle rotated his head with a crack, dropping his small frame with a thud.

"He's out," Spit said definitively.

"Let's stick 'em in one of these," Elise said. Sonny and Isaac each grabbed an ankle dragging the lifeless man into the overhang that Elise lifted. Inside was a teenage Spanish boy, handcuffed on the ground. He jumped at the sound of the door opening.

"We're not going to hurt you," Elise said. In disbelief, tears began to roll down his face. "No, no, no it's okay," Elise tried to comfort him. "Nix, give me your Leatherman," she requested. I handed it to her without input. She manipulated it into a screwdriver. Diving the bit into the keyhole of the cuffs. A few twists and turns the boy's wrist were free. The young man rubbed at his bruises, eyeing us each, studying our motions to decide if he should trust us. Isaac picked up the shackles. He looked deeply at the young boy and said, "Espera aquí, volveremos por ti." The boy nodded back at Isaac, and scooted himself into a shadowed corner.

"They took Lamor." Dani said. We each were stunned into silence.

"It's bad," Freya started. "There's a school just through there and they're holding kids captive. Little kids. They took Dani and Lamor to the back and must have known we were sympathizers. They beat on them pretty good," she said gingerly, touching Dani's arm. "And we think they took Lamor here."

"A little girl said she saw Lynn. She's here somewhere." Dani offered an open hand to the group, showing the headband she had given her. "We gotta find 'em."

"We will," Elise reassured. "Him and Lynn."

Isaac hit my chest and started to jog off. Trickling behind in light jogs, we all collected back to where our search started. "Lynn!" Isaac called out. A thunderous applause broke out in the distance and the pressure of time felt heavier.

"Lynn!" Dani yelled hardily.

The muffled noise came back.

"I hear you, keep making noise! We're coming," Isaac said. The rattled metal clinked and grew louder when we got closer. Landing on the next aisle, storage units were still secured with large locks.

"Lynn!" I hollered from deep within. The rasp of my voice and urgency strained each of my calls.

" Hey girl, I'm here!" Dani pleaded again. The thumps against metal echoed right next to us. We all turned our attention to one particular rusted door. Raising my knee to my chest, I kicked at the door with full force making the lock release itself. Still in pain, Dani fell to her knees scurrying to unlatch it. She pulled the lock off and Spittle helped her push it up. Our eyes grew wide from revelation.

"Lamor!" Freya exclaimed, "Oh God, are you alright?" She entered the small space, pulling at the fabric wrapped around his mouth.

"Just take this shit off of me," Lamor muttered with anger. Spittle whipped out his blade cutting, the knots off the restraints.

"We've gotta get you out of here, you don't look so good," Freya said, helping remove the ties.

"No way, we've gotta get Lynn!" Lamor protested.

" We can't get Lynn and nurse you and Dani along the way. It'll be safer if we get y'all back to the truck." Freya countered. We collectively gave him a once over, his eye was swollen shut and his breaths were shallow. Freya was right, she was rarely ever wrong.

"Lamor, brotha, we've *got* Lynn. We will find her. Please let us help you take care of yourself. You and Dani." I said, acknowledging them both.

"Yea," Elise chimed in. "Let Freya take you both back to the truck. When we get Lynn we'll be ready to roll out," she finished.

Freya squinted in disapproval at Elise. Elise smiled gently at me when she turned her back to them and walked towards me.

Spittle, observing the moment, added, "I'll escort y'all back, we can cut the wire fence over there and make our way to the parking lot without heading through the crowd."

"Nah, I'll go, you stay with them." Sonny gave Spit a firm pat.

"Great, I'll go get the boy," Elise said, beginning to walk off.

We lingered in pairs and trios walking back down the aisle. Applause roared yet again as we rounded the corner. We hovered nearby, watching Elise arm in arm helping the tall teen brace himself. Freya approached them, trading him off. "We'll bring them to the trucks and come right back," she said firmly.

"Get 'em running, we'll be right out," I reassured her. We walked between two units and Spittle kneeled to begin clipping the gate wire.

"Alrighty," Spittle said spreading the gate.

"I'm not going," Dani announced. "I gotta find Lynn," she said. We all knew where she was coming from but still had reservation.

"But Dani." Lamor began to speak for us all.

"I can't sit this out. Lynn and I were close. Are close," Dani said.

Lamor nodded gently. Freya aided the young man out of the perimeter. Lamor and Sonny followed.

"Stay safe," Sonny urged us before departing, "I'll have the truck running and waiting for ya."

Devoted to the mission, Dani lead the charge back down the storage aisle. Our path was interrupted by David's condescension "Are we ready!" He could be heard yelling a few rows over. I shook my head, along with Isaac and Elise. An internal voice demanded I go. Initiating a light jog, we all pressed back to the main square of unfortunate events to come.

A penitentiary style roll out of door releases clanked one after the next. Storage doors rolled up to expose the unlucky victim that stood behind each. Too far to see but close enough for concern, we stayed to bear witness.

"Which offering did you vote for first?" David egged the crowd on. It was like a scene from an ancient Roman play. Watching the barbarian awake in each of the crowd members. They became belligerent with excitement and shouted on as the events continued.

He stood atop their makeshift stage, pointing whimsically. Adding an affirming nod to another man; the crowd cheered at the cue. Without further instruction, the assembly took choppy steps back to increase the circumference around the stage. Gaggles of people thinned into an almost unison line, shoulder to shoulder. We, however, remained aloof behind the action. In seconds it was silent. Heavy footsteps against the ground were the only lingering noise. The MC's man of action, was performing his part. He walked to an unlocked unit and swiftly pulled up the remaining bay door. His keys jingled against each other to open the interior cage.

Here and now, was the return of a deep-rooted ache. Once again, it showed itself and the wash of anxiety consumed me whole. I pressed my eyes together, needing to block it out. Shrill screams, consistent and full, filled the air.

"Nooo! Pleasee!" was screamed through cries of terror. The formation, unwavering, stayed silent.

Her small head was gripped almost entirely in the henchmen's hand, as he dragged her the distance to the stage. Her plea for help bounced off the concrete walls around us. He pulled her upright by her hair, she pulled back, dropping her weight trying to escape.

"No! Let her go!" Dani yelled. The whole crowd directed stares to her.

"Sacrifice is a service. And service comes before self," David encouraged without a wince.

"You kidnapped her. You took her from her home!" Dani screamed with all she could muster. Large men began closing in towards us.

"Lynn, don't worry." Elise called to her. Lynn lifted her flushed face, trying to find her savior in the crowd.

We knew we could only fight our way out. We each drew our weapons and David began to laugh. "It seems we have Uncivil amongst us. Do you see, they are indeed, uncivilized creatures. We are doing great works and they want to introduce violence." The henchmen continued to move, so we followed suit. Standing back to back we took aim, Spittle stood by me, finger steady on the trigger. Clearly outnumbered, my mind skipped reality hoping for a happy ending.

The screaming continued, high-pitched and ominous. The henchmen continued his work, tying Lynn to a post, unfazed by our presence.

"Stop!" I shouted hoarsely across the crowd. A group of men soon became obstacles around us.

"Take me instead," a deep voice bartered. Sonny returned and stood at the aisle entrance in a commanding presence.

"Sonny, no! Nobodies dying today!" Isaac shouted at him. Sonny ignored him and just began walking towards the stage, David's eyes remained fixed onto us.

"She doesn't deserve this," Sonny projected as he approached the henchmen. David still hadn't acknowledged him. The sound and scent of splashed accelerant crept over us. Lynn continued pleading to the man as he doused her in gasoline. Sonny took another step towards the man, his voice now low and direct. I could see Sonny out of the corner of my eye, until I couldn't. Doubled over, inches away from the henchmen, Sonny leaned on to him. The man pulled a blade up and away from Sonny's gut only to dive it in again. Finally pushing him off and unto the ground. My heartbeat thumped into my ears and soon Lynn's screams faded. My cheek absorbed the heat of my bullet casings after each round I released. Squeezing the trigger again and again I watched the path of each bullet enter a skull, a clavicle, and heart. I had to ensure death, not just injury. Chaos ensued, fear took control and the crowd dispersed in all directions.

Collectively moving towards the stage post we each took aim at anyone who approached. The warmth of blood coated me from the blowback of our enemies.

Breaking ranks, Elise sprinted to the stage rushing the man standing guard over Lynn. She rammed her pistol deep into his face, following up with a foot to his groin. Every blow landed in rhythmic sequence.

"Get Lynn!" I yelled at her, my voice sounding distant to myself. I watched Elise begin working Lynn's restraints, before turning to continue where she left off. The henchmen stood upright, trying to accumulate enough strength to strike back. Before he could decide,

I punched the extended clip of my handgun into his temple. Over and over until I sat on top of him, my knees in his shoulder cuffs, striking him relentlessly.

Spittle tugged the back of my collar. "Come on!" was all I heard. Isaac was giving cover to Lynn and we all began to dash for the exit. Scanning and looking back, I could see the pool of blood Sonny laid in. I know it pained us all to leave him in that way. The pressure of our surroundings grew with every moment we remained in this space. Our breaths were out of sync and lacked control, panting along. We turned the corner and dashed in the straightaway. The parking lot was so close. *I just need to make it to Freya.* The heartbeat in my ears slowed. The sound deepened, and slowed. A new heat was accompanied by pain, creating an indescribable void in my back. My heartbeat slowed, the sound deepened. My knees gave into my next step, I stumbled slowly grasping at Elise as I did. The heat spread to my shoulder. The fear in Elise's expression was all I could make out. My shock drowned out their cries for me. Laying there on my back, I looked on while Spittle and Isaac returned fire in the direction we left. Dragging me by my arms and shirt, Elise yelled silent sobs at me jolting me up by my collar.

A horn began to blare, loud, and resounding. A 1 kilohertz tone got my attention like a dog whistle. My conscious drifted between thoughts. I felt light. I thought the natural disaster alerts were no longer operational. Was the unrest over? The sky turned to carpet. The carpet turned into a sunroof. Speeding off, my body rocked in light motions. It was silent. It was calm. I was above it all. Closing my eyes, I can see the Refuge. I think I hear psithurism.